On the Table

Ashley Loren

Published by Ashley Simpson, 2024.

ON THE TABLE

First edition. April 2, 2024.

ISBN: 979-8224660063

Written by Ashley Loren.

Table of Contents

Chapter 1

I roll over in the ruby sheets to find that I'm completely alone in the bed. One disorienting minute passes as I recall that someone had been beside me when I drifted off. The neon glow of the alarm clock in the corner blares eleven. Usually, Mark stays until at least midnight before making the trek back to his own apartment a few blocks over. I force my eyes to focus in the dark and find his shadowy figure at the foot of the bed, sliding on his shoes as quietly as possible.

"You aren't staying," I say without surprise.

"You know I can't spend the night here." He struggles to slip his feet into black sneakers that blend into the inky darkness of the bedroom. Mark makes it sound like he has something to get back to, a lover or a wife. Instead, he refuses to spend the night here because he doesn't like what my mattress does to his back.

"Why don't you help me pick out a new mattress?"

I have some money in savings, probably enough to afford a low-end mattress. It's the sensible thing to do, the responsible thing to spend my money on. Aren't you supposed to replace your mattress every eight years? Mark thinks his sleep suffers on my lumpy mattress; maybe mine does, too.

"I don't think that would be such a good idea." He stands up, his shoes finally on his feet and the rubber soles making echoes on the hardwood floors. His shoulders hunch, and he avoids my gaze as he gathers up his phone, keys, and wallet from the top of the crowded vanity.

"You're a mattress salesman," I laugh. "How are you going to turn away business from a woman who wants to improve her sleep habits?"

"I just don't think buying a mattress is going to solve the problem."

"And what problem might that be?"

"I'm afraid that my spending the night here might give the wrong impression."

I pause, trying to sort out my thoughts and feelings on this. I don't think he has another woman to get back to, but am I wrong? Maybe this was a casual thing for him and he had a steady relationship with someone else full-time. Who *exactly* would get the wrong impression if he stayed? Did he mean me or did he mean another lover?

"It might give the wrong impression to *who*, exactly?" I muster up my courage to ask the question that has been building over the course of the last three months as he sneaks out in the middle of the night every time he comes over.

He hesitates, unsure how to deal with a direct question. We beat around the bush, talking about everything but the things that really matter. Tonight, I'm so tired of this sketchy business of Mark sneaking out in the middle of the night.

"It might give the wrong impression to *you*, Esmerelda."

"And what impression might *that* be?"

"I don't want you to think this is more serious than it is." He slides a hand over his face, as if just having this conversation is exhausting to him. "Spending the night feels like commitment, and we're just here to have a good time."

Mark and I met on a dating app, my first foray into using technology to find a partner. I only joined at Petal's insistence. She claimed my solitary lifestyle was causing me to miss out on a valuable experience. Petal has Jason, and she lured me into the fantasy of going on double dates with the two of them instead of being the third wheel. Mark was the first man I matched with, and we met for drinks at a bar downtown. We talked until midnight over Long Island iced tea and stumbled back to my apartment where he promptly left the minute I drifted off. The first date didn't bother me, but now it was a pattern. He *always* leaves after sex, waiting for me to fall asleep so he doesn't have to say goodbye. What exactly is the issue with him committing for a night when we're already sleeping together?

"I think it's best that you leave," I tell him, throwing back the sheets and standing up to see him out. I want to lock the door behind him, hear the lock snick shut. I want to close this chapter. Dating just isn't for me.

"Don't be upset," he pleads, tucking his wallet into his back pocket. "I'm just telling you how things are. We both knew this wasn't something serious."

I stand by the bedroom door and gesture for him to go out ahead of me. He puts his head down to avoid my eyes as he walks to the foyer of my small apartment. He dealt me an emotional blow, but I square my shoulders like a queen. I can be confident, even in this.

"Have a good night, Mark." I close the door on his bewildered face and lock it behind him. As soon as I know he's gone, I slide down wall and land on the cold tile floor, putting my head in my hands. Part of me wants to cry, but a bigger part says Mark isn't worth the tears. He's just the first boyfriend I've had in two years. Now, I'm not even sure I can call him my *boyfriend*. What did he mean I might get "the wrong idea" if he spent the night here? I press the heels of my hands into my eyes to ward off the impending tears before pushing myself up to stand. There's no way I can go back to sleep now, not with his words echoing in my mind.

Still tired, I slowly make my way toward the clawfoot tub. This tub was the real reason I signed the lease on this apartment. Sure, the setup of the apartment is great and it's convenient to the store where I work. But this clawfoot tub, right in the heart of the guest bathroom, is everything I wanted. Hot water fills the tub and I drop in a bath bomb, watching the soap bubbles rise to the surface. I slip out of my robe and step into the tub, sinking down until only my head remains above the water. The ends of my long hair submerge into the sudsy foam, and I regret not taking a minute to tie it up before climbing in. I close my eyes, feeling the contrast between the cold porcelain of the tub behind my neck and the warm water elsewhere.

What exactly am I doing here with a man who thinks I'll get the wrong idea?

I know what Petal would recommend I do: pull a few tarot cards. My sister is a firm believer in the spiritual aspects of my job and treats it as if it were an exact science. Fortunetelling is an art form, but she believes I have the gift to tell people what they need to hear. She refuses to believe that we use everything on the table to come to a conclusion. The bad news is I don't believe in its magic or power. Still, the tarot deck is a familiar touchstone for me, so I pull my beat-up paperback from beside the tub and thumb through it for a minute. It's an old volume I used to reference when I first started working for Rose in her fortunetelling shop. Every page tells you what it means to read the tarot cards a client might draw. I know the book like the back of my hand. Slipping into the pages feels familiar and comfortable when everything else in my life feels like a trainwreck.

I read a few pages and the discomfort in my body starts to melt away. Finally, I toss the book to the side and simply close my eyes, focusing on the water lapping over my skin. *Mark isn't a serious thing and that's okay*, I tell myself. The point of online dating isn't to find the man I'm going to marry. I should focus on having a good time. I don't want to feel so damn lonely all the time. Somehow, this conversation with Mark leaves me feeling lonelier than ever before.

I sigh and submerge myself completely under the water until my lungs burn. When I come up for air, my hair is dripping around my shoulders and I regret it. I hate going to bed with wet hair because it never dries nicely. A messy bun is about the only option I'll have for my hair in the morning, but it did feel good to have the warm water surround me. It feels like an even trade-off to unwind enough to slip back into an unconscious slumber. With my entire body relaxed, I pull the plug and let the water drain out of the tub. I'm still sitting against the warm porcelain when the last dregs of the water slip away from me. Reaching for the fluffy white towels to my left, I stand up and start to dry myself off. I grab a second towel and twist my hair up in it to avoid dripping all the way back to bed.

Suddenly, I'm far too tired to worry about getting dressed or drying my hair. I stumble into bed still damp and pull the covers up to keep my wet skin warm. As I'm thinking about what it would be like to have a boyfriend after all this time, I drift off into blissful unconsciousness.

Chapter 2

"Let's go for breakfast," Petal says when I pick up the phone. "Is this some kind of sister intuition?"

"No, I'm just craving pancakes with blueberry syrup. You know I hate going out alone, and I happen to know you aren't busy until Rose opens up the shop at eleven." She clicks her nails impatiently against the countertop in her kitchen, like always. It isn't hard to imagine her, leaning over the kitchen island with her chin cupped in one hand. "Come on, sis."

I think about the money I have in the bank account. Petal and I go out all the time, but I never expect her to pick up the tab. She might be my little sister, but the dynamic between us verges on mother-daughter. Ever since our mother died three years ago, there were hard decisions about what I would do to keep our lives on track. Petal has always been a free spirit – as in, she's terrible with money. I would worry more if she wasn't with Jason: steady Jason who pays the bills on time. He's the manager at a car dealership and he makes more than enough to support them both. Still, I don't want Petal to be reliant on a man so I send her money every month and pay when we go out.

Last night filters in like the sunlight through my window. I guess I have more money in the bank now since I don't have to buy a new mattress.

"Breakfast it is," I tell her. "Give me twenty minutes. You're driving."

"You're the best sister in the world," Petal says and hangs up.

"Damn right," I mumble as I throw the covers off. I'm already tying my long hair up and rubbing the sleep from my eyes. Work will likely come straight after breakfast, so I grab something form-fitting and black. Fortunetellers shouldn't be too memorable. It helps set the mood to be a little bit mysterious. Looking the part is important when pretending to tell the future. I finish getting ready, splashing water on my face and brushing on a few coats of mascara.

It feels like no time at all has passed when Petal opens my door. She clicks in with her high heels on and I instantly regret my decision to wear my standard uniform. Petal always manages to look like a million bucks, even if she gets ready at the last minute. Her short hair is smooth and glossy, not a hair out of place. It looks like she just came from the hair salon for her six-week trim. If I didn't know better, I would think she scored that flowing burnt sienna dress from a designer outlet. Instead, it likely came from one of the vintage shops she visits for inspiration. My outfit from Target is probably more expensive than hers.

"Are you ready to go? I'm dying for pancakes," she calls, making her way down the hall.

"So you mentioned." I slip my silver medallion earring in, walking down the hall to the front door. "What's the real meaning behind this impromptu trip if you don't have sister intuition?"

"What do I need sister intuition for?"

"Mark and I broke up last night. I think."

Petal stares at me, waiting for clarification, but I don't offer any. Instead, I grab my keys and toss them into my oversized shoulder bag. I usher her out the front door and into the car.

"What is that supposed to mean?" Petal finally asks, situating herself in the driver's seat while I fasten my seatbelt. "How do you not *know* if you broke up?"

"It turns out our relationship was a little one-sided." I sigh and pick at a piece of lint on my skirt. "*I* thought we were exclusive and *he* thought we were just having a good time. I offered to buy a new mattress so that he would spend the night. Then, he told me I might get the wrong idea."

"What a dick." She reaches over and grabs my hand tightly. "There are more men where he came from on the dating app. And in real life."

"I think I'm done with dating apps."

"You only had one match and it wasn't true love. So what? Get back on the horse and try again." She turns on her blinker and navigates into the parking lot for Jestine's Kitchen.

"I think I liked my life better when there wasn't so much drama."

"It doesn't sound like your night was exactly *dramatic*," Petal corrects. "It was more of a gentle letdown."

"Why don't you tell me what's new with you? I'm tired of talking about my failed love life at the moment."

"I hope we can get a good table," Petal says, gnawing on her bottom lip. "Do you want to sit by the window so we can people-watch?"

I hold the heavy glass front door open for her. Jestine herself greets us at the hostess stand, dressed in the same shade of emerald green that decorates the entire restaurant.

"Ladies," she says, her voice smooth. "It's been a while since I've seen you around here."

"We had a craving for a stack of buttermilks," Petal tells her.

"Should I go ahead and put your order in while you two get settled?"

"If it isn't too much trouble," I tell her.

"Blueberry syrup, please," Petal adds.

Jestine walks us to the small wrought iron table situated below the huge glass window that looks out over the downtown streets. It's early on a Tuesday morning, but there are still plenty of people in Charleston. We watch in silence, completely comfortable sharing the same space. We have always been like this, comfortable with one another. We might be two very different people, but Petal is my safe space, the person I look to when everything else in my life is falling to pieces. She is one of the best parts of my life, especially since our mom died.

"Are you going to tell me what's going on with you?" I ask her when Jestine sets down two plates of flapjacks piled high with butter and blueberry syrup dripping off their crispy edges. Petal spears a bite of pancake and closes her eyes as she chews.

"*This*," she says, "is the real reason why we came out today."

"I have a feeling there's something you aren't telling me."

"You read the future. Why don't you tell me what's going on? *I* thought we were just having a nice sister-date for a change. It feels like it's been ages since I last saw you."

"Petal, we had breakfast together *last* Tuesday."

"Maybe we should make it a tradition."

"How's Jason?"

Petal stares out the window and chews, her expression thoughtful. "He thinks he wants to go back to school, you know – make a career shift. But I don't think this is a good time for that."

Suddenly, this breakfast makes sense. She and Jason must have fought over the future. I don't see why Petal would have told him this wasn't the right time to go back to school. If there was anyone on this planet who had less room to judge when it comes to making a career change, it's Petal. Over the past ten years, she must have held almost two dozen jobs including dog walker, ice cream maker, and now watercolor artist.

"Maybe it's the right time for him," I try to reason with her. "I can't imagine that selling used cars is his passion."

"But it's stable. We need something stable right now."

"Since when have you ever made decisions based on stability?"

Petal stiffens. I made a misstep. She spears a bite of pancake and chews it with vigor. She sets her fork down with a *clink* and looks me square in the eye. "Now isn't the time for upheaval. The cards said so."

I groan. "Please tell me you aren't going to let tarot cards run your life. You know as well as I do that those cards don't mean anything."

"I don't know," she says. "I think there might be something to them this time."

"Why are you being so cryptic and mysterious this morning?"

"What makes you say that?"

"Everything is on the table," I repeat the mantra we use at work. "You're chewing on your lip. You're avoiding my questions. You're making decisions that are totally out of character."

She gives me a small smile. "You always were good at reading people. I wish I could tell you because it would be so much easier. Let's say that you'll find out soon enough. Are you going to finish those pancakes?"

I push the plate toward her and watch as she finishes them. While she devours the last scrap of the single pancake I had left on my plate, I think back to the last time Petal kept a secret from me. Even during the usual times like Christmas and birthdays, she often spoils the surprise days before the actual event comes. I figure that if I just wait her out, she'll eventually spill it.

"You get the check," she says, gesturing toward the bill. "This surprise has left me a little strapped."

I roll my eyes. Whatever she cooked up can't have been too expensive, not on her artist's salary and the money I send her every month.

"I'll pick up the tab this time, but you owe me pancakes next time *I'm* in the mood."

I take the receipt to the front counter and pay, meeting Petal in the car. We drive around the block to my apartment in silence, the tension building between us. She wants to spill the secret, but there just won't be any time between Jestine's and my apartment.

"Call me later?" I ask her as I climb out of the car.

"I'll catch up with you later today." She puts the car in reverse. Just like that, she's gone and the secret is no closer to being divulged.

Chapter 3

Rose and I sit around the tiny table we use when customers come in, but today is a slow afternoon. The table is covered in a black gauzy tablecloth that lays neatly over my legs where I'm pulled into the table. Our lighting is dim and we have candles burning in nearly every corner of the room because it's better for the ambience than bright overhead lights. It's softer and less threatening for telling fortunes and divining the future. People expect mystery, and we do our best to deliver on that promise from the moment they walk through the door.

But today, there are no customers and it's just the two of us.

"Can you believe that?" I ask her, after explaining how Mark left last night.

"I can believe you aren't attracting the right energy to find a partner," Rose corrects me. "It really comes as no surprise that Mark wasn't the one you were after."

"Cut the crap, Rose," I say, a little irritated at her. Rose believes in a way that I don't. "You know as well as I do that 'attracting energy' isn't a real thing."

Rose glares across the table. She hates that I don't believe in telling the future. After all, it's how we make our living. Rose opened this small fortunetelling shop two years ago, bringing me along for the ride. I had no experience telling the future, but she picked me up at a carnival. I was a temp worker manning a booth full of women's clothing. The gimmick was if you bought an item in the shop, I would look into a crystal ball and tell your future. As far as temp work goes, it was the weirdest job I ever had, but I had a lot of fun with it. I read everlasting love and happiness for most people. For skeptics who questioned my ability, I read misfortune: a lost job, an absent partner, a necessary car repair, financial ruin.

Toward the end of the night, Rose came into the tent and started browsing the racks. But what she was really doing was watching me work the room. Eventually, she bought a necklace, the cheapest item in the tent. She brought her receipt to me and sat down in the plush chair across from me. I put my hands on the crystal ball and closed my eyes as if summoning her fortunes directly from the fog in the glass. Taking theater classes in high school paid off that night.

"Tell me: what do you want to know about your future?" I asked, opening my eyes to look at her.

"I don't need you to tell the future," she said. "I'm here to talk about *your* future."

My hands dropped from the crystal ball and I stared at her, dumbfounded. She was the first and only person all night to pose me a question about myself.

"How did you get this gig?" She leaned forward in her chair until only a few inches of space separated her face from mine. It was clear she didn't want anyone to hear our conversation. She need not have worried. By the time she bought her necklace, the only other person in the tent was the cashier. The night was coming to a close and most people were finished with their shopping.

"I'm a temp worker. I take what they give me." My face flushed with the shame of my inability to find a steady job. I hated being a temp worker.

"You have a knack for this, you know. For fortunetelling."

"What good is *that* going to do me in the real world?" I scoffed.

"I could think of something." She smiled and leaned even further across the table. She took my hands in hers. "Come work for me."

"You're offering me a job because I can pretend to read a crystal ball?"

"I'm offering you a job because you have the gift of reading people. I'm opening my own store next week and I could use some help reading tarot cards and even palm reading. You have a gift for telling people what they need to hear. I watched you here, telling people a real story about what comes next for them. You have the gift."

"I'm sorry, but I really don't think that 'gift' is real. I have no idea how to read tarot cards."

"I can teach you. It's something you can learn if you're good at reading people – and you are." She grabbed my palm and flipped it over, tracing the lines with her index finger. "You have great lines on your palm. Let me teach you how to read it."

I took my palm back from her and placed both hands under the table where she couldn't get to them. I stared, not sure what to say or do with this wild woman who wanted me to gaze into a crystal ball for a living. The only problem was, I *did* need a full-time job. Temp working was unreliable and I never knew what I would be doing from one day to the next. Some of these jobs really sucked.

"I don't know," I hedged. "Can I think about it?"

She reached into her pocket and handed me a business card. The weight of the cardstock felt luxurious in my hand and I ran my fingers over the embossed text. Rose Gilbert, I read. Psychic extraordinaire. I laughed out loud at how she marketed herself, but slipped the card into my pocket.

"Call me tomorrow when you're ready to accept the job," she said, rising from the table and grabbing her little gift bag.

As it happened, I called Rose the very next day and accepted her full-time job. I learned the art of interpreting the lines of the palm and she gave me the book I read in the bath last night as I learned to read tarot. Almost two years have passed since that day and I'm still grateful she took a chance on me. Rose is more than just my boss; she's one of my closest friends. I still don't believe in the hippie-dippy mumbo jumbo we espouse to our clients, but I can't argue with how it feels to tell someone good things are coming to them. I learned that it's more about reading a person than the tools we use to tell them what we think.

I shake my head against the memories and try to recenter myself in our conversation.

"All I'm saying is that you're attracting the wrong energy," she says. "If you put positive vibes out into the universe, you would be more likely to attract someone who wants you for *you*, warts and all."

"I don't know how I'm supposed to find someone. Maybe I should just embrace the spinster lifestyle." I shrug my shoulders as if this doesn't bother me.

"I wish I had the answers for you, Essie." Rose looks down at the table and clasps her hands together. "I also wish that I didn't have to deliver more bad news to you on the heels of an almost-breakup."

"*More* bad news?" My stomach sinks as I think about what awful news she could possibly have to tell me. An army of hard marbles lands deep in my gut, sinking lower and lower with every passing second. Rose avoids my eyes and stares instead at her hands. When she does look up, she scans the room and sighs, her shoulders hunching. I start to worry about what else is wrong.

"I'm really sorry to have to do this," she says, taking a deep breath. "I'm closing down the store."

I stare at her, dumbfounded.

"It isn't my first choice," she explains. "Remember when Tony came by the store two months ago and I sent you to lunch? He came by to tell me that rent is going up on our space and I really just can't afford to keep the doors open with the new terms on the lease. I'm going to shut it down and figure out what else the universe has for me."

I study Rose's face for the telltale sign she's bluffing but find nothing there. All I see is sadness that this thing she built is coming to an end. I knew we were barely turning a profit. After all, I help Rose manage the books. The fact that we can't afford a rent hike is no surprise to me, but I'm shocked that her solution is simply to fold her cards and give up.

"Why not find a new location?" It seems like the only logical answer.

"I think this is the universe's way of telling me to move on," she offers. I hate that Rose believes in signs from the universe. "And I'm confident you'll find something else too."

A sly smile crosses her face and I wonder what she knows that I don't. Rose has an uncanny ability to tell what is around the corner, but this feels like more pointed knowledge. If I'm lucky, maybe someone random will offer me a job just like Rose did in that booth. The problem is I'm not sure anyone really *needs* someone to tell their future. Where would I put these skills to good use? I should have spent the last two years polishing my resume rather than reading tarot cards.

"I wish I knew what you're hiding," I tell her.

"All in good time."

My relationship has crumbled, my job is gone, and my best friend and boss is mysteriously promising that the universe has something new in store for me. Whatever it is, it can't be good.

Chapter 4

The following day, I come to work prepared with an army of ideas that could potentially save this shop, our livelihoods, our sense of purpose. I don't know if it's because I'm right on the heels of a non-breakup or if I'm simply more committed to my job than I thought, but I have a long list of options.

"What if we went out into the community and read palms, like I did when you picked me up with that crystal ball?" This is the fifth idea I've pitched, but Rose hasn't bitten on any of them. She simply shakes her head.

"You'll understand why soon enough," she promises. "The universe is about to reveal your next steps."

I notice her attention shift to the parking lot where a silver sedan has just slid into the space directly in front of our door. The woman inside climbs out, her auburn pixie cut catching the sun. *Petal.* She reaches back into the car to grab her phone off the mount on the window before coming through the glass front door.

"I'm going to grab lunch," Rose says suddenly. "Text me what you want from Buddy's." Rose hugs Petal and whispers something in her ear before turning to the parking lot. Petal turns toward me and takes the seat Rose just vacated. She rummages through her cavernous crimson handbag in search of something.

"What are you doing here, Petal? Wasn't breakfast yesterday enough for you?"

"You could at least pretend to be glad to see me." She looks up and sniffs. "I come bearing gifts."

"Well, that's a welcome surprise." I laugh and she pulls a small package out of her bag and tosses it across the table to me. "What's the special occasion?"

"I can't give my sister a gift just because I love her?"

The box is small and slim, wrapped in elegant silver wrapping paper. I pick it up, noting how nothing inside seems to shift around. Whatever it is, it's a solid mass.

"Should I guess what it is?"

"You would never guess in a million years. Just open it."

The wrapping paper comes loose on the ends as I slide my finger under the seam. I make quick work of the paper and reveal a small deck of cards in a white box. "You bought me a deck of cards?"

Petal sighs and grabs the gift from me, opening the cards and fanning them out in front of me. It isn't a deck of playing cards, but rather a deck of tarot cards. Each one features a beautiful watercolor picture that represents the arcana on the traditional Rider-Waite deck. Hands down, it is the most stunning deck of tarot cards I have ever seen. After I look at it for a little while, it suddenly hits me that this is a *handmade* deck.

"Petal, this must have taken you weeks to finish," I say, grabbing the cards from her for a closer look. When I ask her about her painting, she tells me she's doing it professionally and selling it on Etsy. Jason makes enough money to support both of them, so I never really worried she was going to turn into a starving, destitute artist.

"Anything for my sister." She shrugs and relinquishes the deck to me. "But I do have one *little* request. Let me read your cards for you with this deck."

"You know I don't believe that these cards actually work."

"I know *you* don't, but *I* do."

"Did your cards tell you that I'm going to be out of a job soon?" I hand the deck over to her but no surprise flashes across her face. Rose told Petal before she told me. I shouldn't be all that surprised; Rose and

Petal hit it off right away. Petal was often my guinea pig when Rose was teaching me how to read people. They text each other more than either one of them texts me, but it never bothered me until now.

"Just let me read the cards," Petal says. Her nimble fingers are already shuffling the deck. I reach out and take it from her.

"You know I'm supposed to be the one to shuffle if you're going to read for me." I start to mix the cards up, cutting the deck in thirds and placing it back together before handing it over to Petal. She sits up straighter in her chair, her smile beatific as she grabs the cards from me.

"What spread should I pull for you?"

"Why not just keep it simple?" I sigh. "Past, present, future."

Petal nods and pulls the top three cards off the deck, placing them between us on the table. I marvel at the quality of each card: the intricate detail that went into the drawing of each one, the vibrant colors, and the delicate beauty of the rendering. I could never have purchased a deck this beautiful, no matter what I would have spent on it. Not to mention, I know it's one of a kind. Petal's signature adorns the lower righthand corner of each card.

Petal flips over the cards she's pulled, taking a deep breath and closing her eyes to tap into her intuition. Sometimes, I wish I had her faith, her certainty, that these things were really and truly able to divine the future for my clients. It would be nice right about now to have some clarity on my future. I just lost my maybe-boyfriend and my job in the span of 24 hours. What could a tarot card tell me about where I go from here?

"Everything is on the table," I murmur as she starts to read, the familiar mantra to remind her that my story is just as important as the cards themselves.

"The Magician reversed. This card represents your past," Petal says, authoritative as she shifts into the fortuneteller persona. "Ordinarily, this card represents that you have everything you need to bring your dreams to fruition. You have skill and natural talent, creativity, and the power to manifest what you want. Reversed, the Magician means that you lack the confidence to go after your dreams. It symbolizes manipulation and trickery, as well as wasted talent. You need to boost your self-confidence."

"Tell me something I don't already know," I grumble.

"But here's your present: The Tower. It's a time of upheaval for you. There are many uncertainties in your life right now, but you will be able to balance them in the end. You may have to empty your cup to find wealth, success, and contentment. You may have sacrificed truth for convenience, but it is usually a matter of your subconscious rather than a critical decision."

"I can tell this reading is really going to take me places," I mutter.

"Your future still hasn't been determined," Petal huffs, flipping over the third card. "Ah, yes. I can see this one coming true for you. The Fool."

"Fantastic. New beginnings even after I just lost my job and boyfriend."

"The Fool can also mean optimism and adventure," Petal corrects me. "This card holds infinite potential for you, a blank page for your future. There are tons of opportunities out there for you and a new life is around the corner."

I roll my eyes and move to pick up the cards, handing them over to Petal.

"I have a confession to make," Petal says as she shuffles the cards back into the deck. "Rose and I talked about her closing the shop a month ago. She was waiting for the perfect time to tell you. I told her it was time. The perfect time for you to find out what to do next in your life is *now*. Even the cards say so."

"That's all well and good for *you* to say. But *I'm* the one out of a job."

"Well, that's the other part of why I came today. I have a little surprise for you, but we have to make a field trip."

"I'm kind of running the store right now, Petal. I can't just up and leave."

"I don't see any customers here. Rose is already waiting for us. I knew you would be resistant to this idea, so I brought her along for reinforcement." Petal pulls out her phone and pushes the text messages toward me. I read the message from Rose on the screen. *Tell Essie to shut the store down and come with you on this new adventure.*

"I hate it when you two gang up on me."

Petal stands up, slinging her bag over her shoulder. "Maybe you should bring the tarot deck with you. You might want it when we get to our final destination. And I would hate for someone to break in and steal it. I spent a lot of time on those cards."

I slip the tarot deck into my bag but make a mental note to *not* need them, just to prove a point. Petal practically floats to the front door and holds it open for me while I fish out my keys to lock up behind us. Her car beeps as she unlocks it and I slide into the front seat as she gets behind the wheel. I wish she would let me drive.

We make our way out of the parking lot and hang a left at the stoplight, making our way to the downtown district. To my surprise, we don't stop at any of Petal's usual haunts on the strip but instead make our way out of town. She sings along to the radio as we go, with no trace of the nervousness from our breakfast yesterday. I'm not in the mood to make small talk knowing she and Rose have been keeping secrets. Finally, I hear her turn her blinker on and we navigate into a rundown strip mall. The parking lot is pocked with potholes, mostly empty aside from a few cars parked in front of the bar that anchors the strip on the far right.

"We're here," she announces, her voice clear and calm.

"You brought me to a bar in the middle of the day," I assess. There are two other storefronts on the strip, a Mexican restaurant and a nail salon. However, neither of these venues appears to be open at the moment.

"Not the bar, Essie," she chides me. "Open up your eyes and see the future."

I look around the strip and feel dumbfounded at what I'm supposed to be seeing. Nothing here is much to look at and most of the storefronts sit empty. Petal sighs dramatically and climbs out of the driver's seat. I notice Rose's car parked a few spaces down and she, too, climbs out of the car. Realizing that I'm the only one still trying to make sense of what's going on, I climb out.

Petal marches to an empty storefront and takes a small silver key out of her pocket. She turns it in the rusted metal lock on the front door and walks into the abandoned shop. I open my mouth like a guppy, trying to will the words to come. I want this puzzle to make sense. She motions for me to follow her in, Rose trailing a few steps behind me. My eyes adjust to the dim lighting in the atrium and Petal flicks on the lights further back in the building.

Inside, there isn't much to look at. The space looks like it has been vacant for some time. A thin layer of dust covers every available surface and hangs in the air like crystals suspended in the sunlight. The tint on the storefront windows keeps it from letting through much of the natural light flooding the parking lot, giving the room the distinct feel of an abandoned building. The space is mainly one large, open room with space to move around. Two doors line the back wall of the main floor, presumably to smaller office spaces. The entire room is painted the brightest shade of Robin's egg blue I have ever seen, and yet it doesn't create a bright and cheery space. Instead, it looks like the room has tried too hard and still lands on a baby-boy-nursery vibe. With the stale air and the stack of mannequins in the corner, it feels like the place is haunted.

For a moment, I stand in the doorway and survey the space around me. Petal watches me closely, a triumphant smile on her face. It's like she knows I will fall in love with this space. I take a hesitant step away from the front door and further into the room. Upon second glance, I notice the beautiful hardwood floors around the edges of the painting tarps that have been laid out. There are some interesting tables stashed in the corner beneath a pile of mannequins, made of reclaimed wood with an aged appearance. I walk to the middle of the room and spin around to face Petal who is still waiting for me next to the front door.

"You brought me to an abandoned storefront? Are you planning to murder me here?"

"I would never murder my favorite sister." Petal looks directly at me and then glances at the empty room around us. "Use your imagination. I'm solving your problem."

"And what problem might that be, *exactly*?"

"You thought you were going to be out of a job, yes?" Petal rolls her eyes as if I could not be any slower. Still, I can't quite put the pieces together. Rose let me go, leaving me unemployed. Now, the two of them have brought me to a storefront in a rundown strip mall on the outskirts of town. It feels like the answer is right at the edges of my mind, but I can't quite grasp it.

"I'm out of a job and now I'm going to be remodeling this creepy storefront?"

"*We* are going to be remodeling this creepy storefront," Petal corrects me. She abandons her post by the door and comes to stand next to me. She takes my hand in hers like she used to when we were little. "Can't you see it? Do you really have no imagination at all?"

"Rose?" I turn around to face her. Maybe she can fill in the gaps for me.

"We're losing our space," Rose says with a shrug. "I don't have it in me to start a new shop. This one was so hard and I don't want to do it again, but Petal didn't want to let it go. She believes in you."

Finally, the last piece of the puzzle clicks into place.

"Petal." My voice comes out like a snarl. "Please tell me you did *not* lease this creepy storefront in my name."

"Of course not." She smiles again, showing every one of her pearly white teeth. "I leased it in *my* name. We're going to be business partners."

"How could you even *afford* to lease this space?"

"Watercolor painting has really paid off," she says, nonchalant. "Plus, there's the matter of the money you send me every month. Technically, you paid for most of this lease. I could add your name to it, if you want."

My mouth opens. I have a hard time shutting it again. Petal has never been very good at managing her finances, and I worry about her with the unsteady income associated with her art. I don't want to convince her to give up what makes her happy, so I keep her from being a starving artist. I don't send her much; just enough to keep food on the table and maybe pay her utility bill. I know Jason makes enough to cover their rent and pay for most of the bills, but my money lets Petal contribute to their household – or so I thought. How long has she been squirreling it away for this?

"Please tell me that you haven't been saving the money I sent you to do this impulsively."

"Technically, I was saving it for a rainy day. But then Rose told me she was losing her lease and we thought, maybe it was time for you to have something of your own."

Rose looks at the ground, color flooding into her cheeks. "I'm sorry I didn't tell you sooner. I didn't know how to break it to you."

I would be angrier with her if I didn't hear the tears right at the edges of her voice. Instead, I draw my gaze away from an embarrassed Rose and fix my glare on Petal. There is no way she would have done something like this without consulting me first. There has to be a way out of this.

"We *can't* do this, Petal." I try to reason with her. The stubborn set of her jaw says she isn't going to hear what I have to say. "I don't have any experience running a business and I need to find a job that actually *pays* me."

"Don't be so modest," Rose volunteers. "You've been running my shop for the past year so I could step out of the leadership role. You're ready for this, Essie."

"There has to be some way out of this lease. If you would just let me talk to the realtor—"

"I signed the lease at the attorney's office this morning," she cuts me off, but her cheeks are taking on a pink color. "Besides, I don't think you're going to want to talk to the realtor."

"You didn't." I growl. Petal places her hands up and takes a step back from me. I haven't wanted to pounce on my little sister since we were kids, but I'm ready to lunge at her now. "Tell me you did *not* call my *ex* to lease a storefront so that I can *pretend* to be a psychic."

"He's the best realtor around. He made sure we got an awesome deal on this place."

"You got an 'awesome deal' on this place because it's in a shitty strip mall and is one of the creepiest places I've ever seen."

"Use your imagination, Esmerelda." She rolls her eyes. "Rose, can you see the space?"

"Esmerelda, you know this space would be perfect with a little work. We could cut down on the creepy vibes just by tossing those old mannequins in the corner. Hell, we could probably sell them and help cover the cost of remodeling."

"Picture it: these old wooden tables in the center of the room. Rose already said we could have the chairs from her place for a steal. All this place needs is a deep clean. And a definite fresh coat of paint. There are even two office spaces in the back: one for you and one for me."

"And of course, I'll come on to help out when you need me," Rose volunteers.

"I can't do this," I hiss at Petal. "I can't believe you would do this without even talking to me first."

"I knew you would never approve, but you would hate to see the money for the lease go to waste now that it's been bought and paid for. Now, you have no choice."

"I most certainly *do* have a choice." I turn back toward the front door. "Rose, will you take me back to the store?"

"Of course," she says. "Why don't I give you two a minute alone and you can meet me in the car in a few?" She backs out of the front door and I watch her hurry through the potholes and into the driver's seat of her forest green sedan.

"You had *no* right to do this," I turn to Petal. "I'm going to get us out of this mess."

"It's a done deal," Petal beams at me. "But you can do what you need to do to accept that. Let's lock up behind us. We wouldn't want anyone to steal our mannequins."

She ushers me out the front door and sticks her key in the lock behind us. The lock sticks, so she jiggles it up and down a few times before turning it over. I hear the tumblers click into place as she stands up straight and slips the key back into her huge bag. She practically dances her way back to the car. I follow her, angry at how happy she is. Meanwhile, my life is collapsing around me.

"When you're ready to start remodeling, let me know." She slips into the driver's side door and I turn my back to walk to Rose's car.

"I'll never be ready to remodel this place," I mumble, but she can't hear me. The door is already shut. She gives me a jovial wave and backs out of the parking spot.

"Have an open mind," Rose says when I get in the car.

Right now, the only thing I can think about is what I'm going to have to do to get Petal out of the financial obligation to pay for this place. There is no way she could have secured a lease on her artist's salary and the small sum of money I send her every month. A lease, even in this shabby strip, would leave her strapped for the next year. *A year*. She must have signed this lease for an entire year. I start doing the math in my head to calculate what it must have cost.

There's no way around it.

I'm going to have to call Turner.

Chapter 5

"Golden Key Realty." A chipper female voice answers. I picture her as tall and elegantly dressed with expensive makeup. "How can I help you?"

"I need to speak to Turner Rodham," I tell her. "Please."

The phone line clicks as she transfers me to Turner's office. It begins to ring and I think, for just a moment, about hanging up the phone before he picks up. Is Petal's idea the very worst thing in the world right now? Calling Turner certainly seems to take the cake on the list of awful things I have to do right now.

"This is Turner." His voice sounds exactly as I remember it: smooth as velvet and soft.

"We need to talk about Petal," I tell him.

"Ess," he says, surprise coloring his voice. He's the only one who has ever gotten away with shortening even my nickname to a single syllable. "Did she finally give you her surprise? I have to say, I was a little surprised when she called me."

"Yes, she gave me a surprise," I bite back. "How could you let her do this?"

"Petal is a grown woman, Esmerelda. She can make her own decisions about where her money goes and what she wants to do. Who am I to stand in her way when she wants something?"

I bite my bottom lip to keep from screaming into the phone. Turner should know by now that Petal often acts on impulse. It's why she flits from job to job, always quitting at the last possible minute.

This is an expensive mistake she hasn't thought through – much like everything in her life. How can he not see that?

"I just need to know what we can do to get out of this lease."

"I'm sorry, but I truly can't help you there."

"You helped her sign this lease. Now, I need you to help her get out of it." I sense my voice rising and I make a mental effort to keep my tone more neutral. This might not be something I can undo for her, tying us together in a way I'd prefer not to experience.

"The ink is dry on the contract." He hesitates a moment. "And she already paid in full."

"She paid for a year-long lease in cash?" I can't help but feel surprise. The idea that my sister could have saved enough to pay for a commercial lease in full is shocking. She isn't depending on this new business to make money to cover the cost of the lease. What is she up to?

"Well, she paid with a cashier's check but it's pretty much the same thing."

"How did she have enough cash to do that?" I catch myself wondering aloud, but I already know Turner has no answers for me.

"She's not the same helpless little girl you seem to think she is," Turner corrects me. "She really seems like she's gotten her life together the past couple of years. A steady boyfriend, a good job. Now, she wants to return the favor of looking out for you like you did for her all those years. Is that really such a bad thing?"

"I don't *want* to run a shop."

"Maybe give it a go. I know I would come visit you for a reading."

Suddenly, the only thing I can picture is being in the same room as Turner. We would sit across from each other at one of those tiny wooden tables. Maybe our hands would brush as I passed him the tarot deck to cut and transfer his energy to the cards. It would be warm and electric, just like it had always been between us. I shake my head to set those images free in order to focus on the conversation.

"There's really *no* way to get her out of this lease?"

"Not unless you want to hire a lawyer," he muses. "And even then, it seems unlikely. Petal knew what she was doing, waiting until things were official before she told you. She's been looking at this place for weeks."

That draws me up short. It's unlike Petal to do anything that requires planning. She must have known from the moment Rose found out she was losing the shop – which makes me angry at Rose. Still, Petal being able to keep a huge secret from me is astounding. It makes me wonder what else she might be hiding.

"I know this isn't what you want to hear," Turner says. "But I think you could be great at this."

"You've never had a reading in your life," I find myself almost laughing. We haven't spoken in two years, but here we are. Petal couldn't have planned this better if she tried. "You have no idea if this is something I'm good at."

"You're good at everything you do. I believe in you. I think you should take Petal up on her offer."

"Thanks for the free advice," I tell him, my voice dripping with sarcasm. "And thanks for taking care of my sister."

"When you open the doors on your shop, let me know. I'd like to come and see the place when it isn't so spooky with all those mannequins in the corner."

I catch myself laughing. Of course, Turner would have the same idea that I did on the vibe of the storefront.

"It *is* a little creepy, isn't it?"

"It's majorly creepy," he says. "Definitely some spirits in there. Petal told me you read the future, but maybe you could start doing seances too."

Suddenly, it feels like we're back to our old familiar banter. I need to end this phone call here and now before I wind up hurt again.

"Well, thanks for nothing, I guess," I tell him. I try to keep my voice light, but the reality is I'm disappointed he can't do more to help me out of this bind.

"Let me know when you open the doors." A pause fills the line, but neither of us hangs up. I hear him take a deep inhale before he says, "I'd love to see you in action."

"I'll keep you posted," I say, having no intention of doing that in the slightest. I click off the call before I have an opportunity to say anything else that might make this phone call hurt more than I know it will later tonight.

Turner and I haven't spoken since we broke up two years ago. He was there for me when my mom died, but he didn't agree with how I chose to shelter Petal in the aftermath of her death. He thought Petal was an adult who needed to learn to fend for herself and stop being so reliant on everyone else all the time. I was trying to keep her afloat financially and emotionally. It makes sense he would allow her to do this now, without my consent or knowledge. Turner always thought Petal was capable of more than I gave her credit for, and he would have thought this new business venture proved how clever she was.

I toss my phone onto the desk in Rose's back office and bury my face in my hands. Without thinking, I scream into my palms hoping that it will muffle the sound in case there are clients. A moment later, Rose appears in the doorway, her eyes soft and sympathetic.

"No luck getting out of the lease?"

I shake my head. "How could you let her do this?"

"It might be hard for you to see right now, but Petal really thought this through. She has a plan, and I think maybe you should let her take care of you for a change. You can do this, Essie. I know you could be just as successful on your own as I've been here."

"I don't *want* to be successful," I moan. "I'd rather just go back to temp work."

"Somehow, I don't really believe that."

"It would be preferable to the stresses of running a business."

Rose laughs. "You basically run my business now. The only thing you don't do is count the cash in the drawer at the end of the night. Maybe you can push that responsibility off on Petal when you run your place."

"It's a huge commitment," I argue.

"But the commitment has already been made," Rose says. Her voice takes on a different quality, and I recognize it as the voice she uses when she's reading tarot cards.

"Why is everyone ganging up on me?" I whine.

"Maybe we just have a clearer view of what's best for you." She looks at me with sad eyes. "I'm sorry we have to shut the store down here and that you're in this position you don't want to be in. But you have to admit that Petal's timing is impeccable and this could be the next opportunity you need to make a good living. Why don't you take the rest of the afternoon off and think about it?"

"Are you going to be okay here on your own?" Already, I feel the freedom that comes with a rare afternoon away from the shop. Petal has consumed most of my week between breakfast and this latest excursion. I could use some time just for myself, even if all I do is clean up my place.

"This store is on its way out. I'm not concerned with great customer service at the moment. Not to mention, I don't exactly see people beating down our doors."

I nod and head to grab my bag.

"Don't forget your tarot deck," Rose says, handing me the beautiful watercolor set Petal made for me. I might be angry, but this deck of cards is could become my favorite belonging. "I think there's something special about this one."

I roll my eyes and toss the deck into my bag. We always have customers who try to make off with our cards, as if the cards are the most important part of the reading. They have no idea the theatrics that go into making this an experience they will never forget. We use everything we see to give a personalized card reading – and it often has very little to do with the actual cards we draw. Still, people think the decks are the magic of the whole thing. I would hate to lose this from a client walking off with it.

"Try not to burn the place down," I try to say as I back out the door. My laugh sounds false, too frantic and loud. Rose is so good at reading people; I know she'll pick up on the note of hysteria and report it to Petal later.

I walk through our parking lot, taking note of the differences between this and the storefront where Petal brought us. Thinking about that location as *my* store doesn't feel right because I have no intention of opening my own shop. Even so, the parking lot here is smooth, and freshly paved just a few years ago. We don't see an inordinate amount of traffic, and the pavement is preserved for the most part. A few cracks line the stalls directly in front of the doors. It's a far cry from that pothole mess in the rundown strip mall for a store that has definitely seen better days.

I sit in the driver's seat of my car and stare at the lavender building that has housed so much growth over the past two years. Truly, the building is perfect for a shop like Rose's. The façade resembles a quaint cottage with ivy growing up one wall and an exposed brick foundation. The landscaping and its evergreen shrubbery look like we spend hours tending to the greenery even though landscapers only come once every three months to trim things up. This property beckons people in while the new one—*mine*, if I want it to be—warns people away. I sigh and try to turn my attention to problem-solving.

As I navigate through town back to my apartment, I feel an inexplicable draw to the cards Petal made me, beckoning me from my bag. Even on my best days, I have no sentimental attachment to the tarot deck. It's a tool we use to divine the answers to our client's questions, but it isn't the most important part of the reading. Instead, we look at the whole person: the way their hair is styled, whether they have their nails done, and how much baggage they bring with them to the appointment.

Rose has a saying she used frequently when I was training: everything is on the table. It means that you need to take a look at the whole person, every detail of their lives, before you interpret the cards. Tarot is a subjective thing even in the hands of an expert. The way someone presents themselves to the meeting, the eagerness in their eyes to hear the future – it all makes a difference in how we read their cards. Body language is even more important than the cards we pull because it shapes the divination.

Even though I know that reading tarot is more or less a sham, I know I will go home and pull my own cards with this new deck. I drive the few blocks back to my apartment and let myself into the silent space. With my bag hung up on the hook and flats slipped off by the front door, I grab the tarot deck and make my way to the dining room table. It was an expensive splurge when I got this apartment, made from reclaimed wood in a farmhouse style. I pictured hosting dinner parties here, but I never made enough friends to warrant an oversized table like this. Now, it reminds me of the abandoned tables in the new location. A deep sigh escapes as I stare down at the tarot cards in front of me.

I take my time flipping through them, admiring the artwork on each one. Petal has certainly developed her artistic talents since the last time I saw her work. The cards are incredibly intricate, delicate, and colorful. Every single card has a beautiful illustration, even the ones I know I would hate to pull for myself. Eventually, I decide to read my cards and shuffle the deck with my eyes closed. I make every effort to transfer my energy to the deck–whatever that means–and focus on the question in my mind: *what should I do with my future?*

When I feel like the deck is ready, I pull the top card off the stack and flip it face up on the table: Eight of Cups.

This can't be right.

This card signifies I have a new beginning ahead of me, but it can't possibly mean I need to open my own shop. It could also mean bravery, leaving something behind to embrace a new beginning. Eight of Cups tends to mean that you can't go back to the way things were before. Disgusted with myself for even attempting to tell the future with these cards, I push them aside and push away from the table. Nothing makes me feel better than deep-cleaning my apartment. I grab my caddy of cleaning supplies, flip my upbeat music onto the speakers, and start in on the bathroom. With the whole afternoon in front of me, I can get to every room in the apartment.

As I shake the Comet from its can into the bathtub, my phone rings from the dining room. I think about ignoring it for a moment but worry it might be Rose calling me back to the store. The cleaner needs to sit in the tub for a couple of minutes anyway, so I double back to grab the phone. An unknown number.

"Ess?"

You have got to be kidding me.

"I think you've done enough damage for one day, don't you?"

"I know you aren't happy about what Petal did for you, but it wasn't my place to tell her not to do this. I'm a real estate agent. It's literally my job to sell and lease properties."

"What do you want, Turner?"

"Meet me for dinner."

"And *why* would I want to meet you for dinner?"

"Because I'm the only one who knows what Petal was thinking when she made this choice on your behalf. I have the information you want, and I want to see you. After two years, don't you think we can bury the hatchet and have dinner like two civilized grownups?"

I curse under my breath because I know he's right. I *do* want to know what Petal thought she was doing when she rented this space. She would never tell me and I know that asking her is futile. My mind drifts to the cleaner in the bathtub, the sheets that need washing to clean Mark right out of my life, and the floors that desperately need to be mopped. Turner is possibly the last person I want to see right now, but I find myself agreeing anyway.

"Let's meet at Jestine's," he says, taking my silence for acquiescence.

"I've already been there this week. Bad memories," I tell him. "King's is better."

"Meet you there at 6:00." He hangs up the phone and I'm left staring at a blank screen. I can't believe I just agreed to meet my ex for dinner.

Chapter 6

I spend an hour scrubbing every corner of my apartment. It feels a little more like I'm attacking it rather than improving it, but it was a great distraction from tonight. Now that I was solidly in the process of getting ready, I had too much time on my hands to think about what I was about to do. Turner and I have no business meeting up, and yet I can't explain why I thought this dinner would be okay. I want to know what Petal was thinking, but could Turner deliver on that promise?

Instead, my mind drifted to the reason we broke up in the first place. We had been together for three years and I genuinely believed we were on the path toward marriage, something a bit more permanent. Then, my mom died and Petal needed me more than ever before. He wanted us to take the next step in our relationship, but I was barely treading water at home trying to pick up the pieces after mom died while taking care of Petal. I couldn't move in with him. I knew logically that Petal was a grown woman now and she could take care of herself, but I couldn't bring myself to abandon her. Petal was still living at home with our mom, taking care of her in the final days of her battle with cancer. After she passed, I moved in with Petal to our childhood home, and we hunkered down through the storm of our grief.

Turner told me he thought Petal could manage the house on her own, that she would want to move on from the life she had as a caretaker. He implied that I should too. After waiting around for weeks for me to make a final decision, Turner gave me an ultimatum: choose between him and my sister. It comes as no surprise that I chose Petal. Six months later, she decided to move into her own place and I sold our mom's house—with a different real estate agent. The damage between Turner and me had already been done and there was no reparation on the table. I thought about him many times over the past two years, but I never reached out to him. I assumed he moved on with his life.

And yet, here we were about to have dinner together and talk about – of all things – Petal.

I navigate to the restaurant in a daze. With a few efforts, I parallel park along the curb and stare up at the restaurant front. I can't make out the people inside the restaurant because of the reflection of light from the street. I picture Turner somewhere inside already, watching the street for my arrival. I curse under my breath, grab my bag, and slam the door of the car shut. As I approach the restaurant, I see Turner waiting outside, hands in his pockets. He looks casual, as if we go to dinner like this all the time. Leave it to him to be cool and collected while I'm a nervous wreck. I feel one major event away from a panic attack. I wonder how he feels about sitting down with me after our relationship ended so abruptly – and on not-so-great terms.

"You came," he says when he spots me. His eyes appraise me, traveling up and down my body. I'm glad I opted for something other than my usual work attire. At least I look halfway decent to make him question his decision.

"Did you expect someone else?"

"It's been two years since we even spoke. Forgive me for wondering whether you would stand me up when you agreed to meet me."

Already, we are off to an auspicious beginning. Our argument sparks as soon as I walk up. It feels like no time has passed since we broke up. This was the way it was at the end, erasing the precious memories of when we used to be good together. I know I'm partly at fault and responsible for my role in our breakup, but it doesn't seem fair for him to still be nursing this grudge so many years later. Not to mention, *he* invited *me* to this dinner.

"I'm sorry," he says, running a hand over his face. "I didn't mean for it to come out like that. I'm really very glad you came."

"Should we go inside?" I ignore both his outburst and his apology because it feels like there is nothing to say. His remark about my arrival was justified, but I don't want him to think he has to apologize for it. I wonder if it's possible for us to turn this evening around.

He holds the door open for me and walks confidently up to the hostess who gives him an appraising glance before casting her attention onto me. I'm used to this sort of glance, the one that says I'm not worthy of his company. Turner is fit and trim, handsome and confident enough in his appearance to stand taller than his six-feet-three-inches. On the other hand, I tend to fold into myself in an attempt to be made smaller. My beauty is ordinary at best. We look like an odd coupling.

I correct myself: we are *not* a couple.

As we sit down at the table, Turner slides his menu to the side. We've both been here often enough to know we will order the cheese ravioli with extra parmesan cheese on top. He folds his hands in front of him and waits for me to say something. I put the ball in his court. After all, he invited me here. He must have something to say. I relish the feeling of control.

"Petal showed you the storefront today," he starts.

"I suppose I should give you a big thank you for letting her spend so much money on some harebrained scheme."

"I don't think you're giving her enough credit. She spent weeks scouring listings, looking for the space that really 'resonated' with her. Her words, not mine."

"You have been helping my sister look for *my* business for *weeks*, and nobody thought to include me in this plan?" The anger drips off each one of my words, bitten to a short staccato. This dinner was a bad idea.

"What's done is done," Turner finally says. "I think you should hear why Petal decided to do this for you."

I stare across the table at him, refusing to take the bait.

"You must be at least a little bit curious about why Petal would do this. Otherwise, I can't think of a single reason why you would come to dinner with me tonight. Admit it – you don't understand what she did and you want some help."

"Fine," I finally respond. "Tell me what she was thinking."

"She was thinking that you had great potential to do something more than you were doing. When your boss told her that she was closing down her shop, Petal immediately called me and we started talking about what she wanted in a space."

"Once again, I want to point out that I was kept in the dark here. I didn't even know Rose was closing her shop until yesterday."

"Ess, Petal isn't as helpless as you seem to think she is. Do you want to know how she paid for that space?"

"I assume you're going to tell me whether I want to know or not."

"She's been saving every single check you send her in a separate account. Petal knew she didn't want your money to support herself and needed a way to return it to you. This was the only solution she could think of – that the two of you could build something together."

"She wants to build a store *together*?"

"She didn't tell you that?"

"Well, I was so angry when she brought me to that creepy place and sprung this on me that we didn't really talk about what her vision was for the space. I didn't know that she wanted to be a part of helping with it. It feels like an added responsibility when I'm already juggling so many moving pieces."

"Petal has really come into her own since we were together," he says, his expression more thoughtful. "I remember when she was that lost and lonely kid, depending on you for everything. Now, she's a business owner and an artist." He pauses. "It's a shame that her boyfriend didn't work out, but it was good to know that she was capable of having a steady relationship. She used to be so flighty."

"What do you mean – that her boyfriend didn't work out?"

"You know, the breakup. It was probably like six weeks ago, right around the time we were starting to look for your property. She seems to have rebounded fairly well. Petal always was more resilient than you gave her credit for."

"I didn't know they broke up." My voice is almost a whisper. How could Petal not have told me that she and Jason were no longer together? Panic sweeps over me at the idea that Petal no longer had that financial safety net and had spent thousands of dollars on this lease.

The waitress came to take our orders and we fell into companionable silence. I'm too busy reflecting that Petal would keep something so monumental from me. I saw her twice this week, giving her ample opportunity to tell me. Breakfast would have been the ideal time to share her relationship with Jason had gone off the rails. Instead, she told me Jason went to work and that was why she needed me to go get pancakes with her. What was she thinking?

"Tell me what you've been doing the last couple of years," Turner finally says. His gaze lands on me and I feel my face flush.

"I'm sure you already know that I made a career change. No more temp work for me."

"I did hear something about that, yes." He smiles. "Explain to me how it came to be that you – the woman who approaches everything with logic and reason – started to tell fortunes for a living."

I regale him with the tale of Rose finding me in the booth at the fair, reading my fake crystal ball. Even I have to admit, this story seems unlikely and yet is completely true. How *did* I get from there to here? It seems like no time at all has passed between us when the waitress comes by to set our food on the table.

"Enough about that," I say, taking the first warm bite of the cheese-stuffed ravioli. "How is business? I see you're doing what you always dreamed of doing."

He fills me in on how he got his real estate license, the types of properties he finds, and the stories of his best customers. Our conversation flows easily and smoothly. You would never know we had a nasty breakup all those years ago, would never know that we hadn't spoken in two years. Now, we find ourselves here at this table. When the waitress brings the check, he immediately takes it and pays. I rummage around in my purse for cash to leave a tip for the waitress, contributing something to the meal he insists on paying for.

As we walk out of the restaurant, he places a hand on the small of my back. His skin on the thin fabric of my dress radiates heat and I have to admit it feels good. Just as quickly, he seems to think the better of it and removes his hand.

"I parked around the block in the garage," he says, stopping in front of my car. "I wasn't lucky enough to find front-row parking."

"Thanks for dinner," I tell him. "I don't forgive you for going behind my back with Petal, but it was nice catching up with you."

"Think about what Petal is trying to do for you instead of focusing on the fact that she went around you to do it. She knew you would never agree, but she's giving you a great opportunity. I hope you decide to take it."

I click the remote on my car to unlock the doors and stand there awkwardly with Turner, not sure what the appropriate goodbye is. He seems just as uncertain as I am, but he reaches out and brushes his warm fingertips along my cheekbone.

"I hope you'll stay in touch," he says, drawing his hand back.

"I guess we'll see," I tell him, trying to be noncommittal and not let on what his touch has ignited in my body. "If I need a second location, I'll keep you in mind. Maybe you and Petal can start planning for a chain of Esmerelda's Fortunes."

He throws his head back and laughs. "You haven't changed a bit. Have a good night, Ess."

With that, he walks away from me and leaves me at my car. I watch him for a moment, his back fading as he progresses down the block and eventually around the corner. I can't believe we just had dinner together, and I feel alive in a way Mark never managed to ignite in me. I shake my head and climb into my car, navigating home. He gave me a lot to think about. But for now, I need to plan out how I'm going to confront Petal with everything I learned tonight.

If she thinks I'm going to just go along with this harebrained attempt to force me into doing this, she has another thing coming.

Chapter 7

I pull up to Petal and Jason's townhome before I realize I don't even know if Petal still lives here, not now that Turner told me they broke up. This townhome belongs to Jason. Petal moved in with him around their one-year mark. If anyone was going to leave the house, it would be Petal. Having no other options, I trudge up to the front door and ring the doorbell. While I do, I observe the beautiful garden Petal worked so hard on in the front yard. It's filled with the dark green spikes of the sego palms and thriving azalea bushes, though they aren't in bloom at the moment. I ring the doorbell again, impatient to confront Petal with what she has been hiding from me.

"Esmerelda," Jason greets me, swinging the door wide open. I look past him into the house, searching for a sign of my sister. "What can I do for you tonight?"

I shift my gaze from the inside of the house and my eyes land on his face. His eyes are red, bloodshot. His usually clear skin looks blotchy and red. Some of the anger drains from me. Jason was the closest thing to a brother I had, and he is clearly struggling with the news of this breakup. His red-rimmed eyes tell me it wasn't exactly a mutual parting.

"I'm looking for Petal," I tell him. "Is she here?"

He moves back from the doorway and gestures for me to come inside. Stepping into the foyer, I see the rest of the house more clearly than I could from the doorstep. The far edges of the living room are lined with cardboard boxes in various states of being packed. Turner was right – they did break up and now I'm walking into the debris of their fractured relationship.

"Petal," I call out. At the sight of the boxes, my anger is rekindled. How could she possibly do this to her life – and mine?

"There's no need to shout." She pops her head around the corner of the living room at the sound of my voice. "I'm right here. Did you come to tell me that you've changed your mind?"

"I came to see what the hell is going on here," I correct her.

"I'll leave you two to it," Jason says, backing away and starting on the stairs. I'm sure he wishes he had somewhere else to go. He's always been a little conflict-averse.

Petal sighs and waves for me to come to the living room. She sinks into the sofa and crosses her legs neatly beneath her, lithe and agile. I've always been jealous of the way she moves with such ease and grace. I remember why I'm here when I look up and see all the boxes with her name on them.

"I just came from dinner with Turner. And you'll never *believe* what he shared with me."

Petal flinches and looks at the floor.

"How could you not tell me something was wrong?"

"I didn't know how to tell you my life was falling apart," she shrugs. "You worry so much about me, and I didn't want to add to your stress. I wanted to do something *for* you – for *us*, really. When Rose told me she was shutting her place down, it made sense that I could provide something new for you."

A pause settles between us.

"Did you really have dinner with Turner?" she asks, her face lighting up.

"It was dinner, Petal. It's not like we ran back to my apartment and shucked off our clothes."

"Remember what the cards said. That you would find love in an unexpected way. The Magician reversed, remember?"

"I don't need to remind you that tarot cards don't *actually* tell the future." I roll my eyes. "Can we talk about the fact that you and Jason are calling it quits and that I just came into your house to see your things all in boxes?"

"The future is uncertain," she says mysteriously.

"Please tell me you did *not* make this decision after reading your tarot cards."

"Of course not. It was a long time coming. We just aren't as compatible as we thought we were. I'm going to be okay, Essie. I promise."

"Then can we talk about what you were thinking when you leased this shop?"

Petal sighs and pulls her knees into her chest, wrapping her arms around them. She looks like a small child folding in on herself, trying to become truly and completely invisible. I don't give her what she wants, staring harder until she finally clears her throat and answers.

"You saw the tarot cards I pulled for you earlier today. Your future was unclear when Rose decided to close up shop. I did this for you so that you didn't have to go back to temp work. I know how much it drained the life out of you. You weren't meant for short-term work."

"Are you really trying to convince me that this was totally and completely for my benefit?"

"Well, I thought I might move my art studio into one of the back rooms and could help you run it. I need something to do with my time now that Jason and I are done. But the store is *mostly* for you."

She avoids looking me in the eye. It becomes obvious this was a desperate attempt to get what she needed most: a touchstone, something that was hers in the midst of losing so much that never really belonged to her in the first place. She no longer has her studio in the upstairs bedroom with the beautiful natural lighting. In fact, Petal doesn't even have a place to live as far as I know. I make a mental note to ask her and help her plan for a move, but I won't touch on it now. This store is her way of trying to bring us back together, to give herself something she can rely on in the uncertainty. In an instant, all of the anger and bravado that filled me on her doorstep slowly melts and dissipates.

"Do you really want to do this, Petal?"

She nods.

"Do you realize how much work is going to be involved in getting a store up and running? It's going to mean long hours and lots of grunt work. I helped Rose get her shop off the ground, and it wasn't smooth sailing."

Petal brightens at the talk of opening the store. Her head snaps up at this change in tone, and she looks me in the eye for the first time since we sat down.

"Does that mean—"

"Well, you already paid for the lease in full and Turner doesn't seem to think there's any way out of it. We might as well give it a go so that we don't waste your investment."

She squeals and launches herself across the couch and into my lap, her arms tangled around my neck. Her hugs are fierce, full-body affairs. I expect nothing less. I wrap my arms around her and breathe in the floral scent of her shampoo and hair products.

"Petal, I love you but don't *ever* do anything like this again."

"Thank you, thank you, thank you," she says in response. "You have no idea how much I needed this."

"Can we talk about what's going on here with you?"

"Maybe tomorrow," she says. "I really need to finish packing."

"Petal, I wish you would let me in. I can't help you If I don't know what's going on."

"I don't need any help, Essie," she says. "This shop is going to be a good thing for us."

I get up off the couch, aware that Petal wants to be left alone with this celebratory news. She might be celebrating, but I feel like I need a glass of wine. I can't believe I just agreed to con more people out of their money, telling them that I can read their fortune from the lines that cross their palm or from a deck of cards. What was I thinking?

Chapter 8

I'm absentmindedly shuffling my new deck of tarot cards while Rose finishes up with one of her regular clients. When I watch her work, I sometimes can't believe this *isn't* a real science. Rose swoops people up in her mysterious persona until the regular Rose hardly seems to exist at all. From the corner of my eye, I watch her closely with the old woman in front of her. The woman is tense, sitting on the edge of her seat while Rose holds her palm between her hands. She has a lock of box-dyed brown hair hanging into her eyes, but she is too absorbed in the reading Rose is giving her to pay it any mind. Her body is pitched forward as if she were ready to dive across the table as soon as Rose opens her eyes.

"Yes, I see it more clearly now," Rose intones as she rubs her fingers over the woman's palm. Kelly, I think her name is. "You are going through something difficult, yes? But the fates seem to be telling me you will prevail, triumphant and stronger than before. See this line here?"

Rose is never shy about telling her secrets to the clients. In fact, I think it's the reason why so many of them come back. They trust in the art of the reading, believing there is a real science behind our predictions. I make a mental note to be more proactive in telling my own clients what they want to hear. Maybe I would have more regulars if I pointed out the depth of a life line etched across their palm.

My mind flickers to the idea that I may have a chance to prove this philosophy works. After last night with Petal, I feel locked into the nebulous concept of opening my own shop alongside Petal. I take a deep gulp of air and try to swallow the nausea that rises up when I think about what's waiting around the corner. I gulp too loudly and Rose opens her eyes just slightly, casting her glance over at me. I mouth that I'm sorry, Kelly's back to me so that she can't see the interaction.

"Your life line is strong," Rose finishes as she stands up slowly from the table. "You have nothing to fear with this challenge in front of you. Based on your palm, I'd say there may even be love in the cards for you." Rose laughs. "Maybe we should pull your cards next time you come."

The woman hands her the cash for her reading and Rose walks over to put it in the register.

"Thank you again, Rose," Kelly says as she backs out of the shop. Rose turns to me, almost triumphant.

"I heard you made a decision on the shop," she says, looking like the cat that ate the canary. "I knew you wouldn't be able to turn down the opportunity to really work for yourself. Me, I'm tired of it. But I think it would suit you."

"Do you and Petal discuss me exclusively when you talk?" I roll my eyes. "Lately, it seems like I'm the only one left out of the conversation. You knew about the store; you knew about my decision. You probably even knew about Jason."

"Jason?" Rose furrows her brow until a little divot appears between her eyebrows. "What about him? Did he get a promotion?"

"They broke up."

Her eyes widen and she places a hand on her heart. "But they were so good together. What in the world would have happened to make them break up?"

"I wish I could tell you. I went by their house last night and all of Petal's things are in boxes in the living room. We didn't get much of a chance to talk about where she was going next. Jason was home. I didn't want to talk about him in front of him, you know?"

"I think we should stage an intervention," Rose announces. "Let's see what the cards have to say."

"Maybe we should just pick up the phone and call her. I don't know if tarot cards are going to tell us how to make her fall in love with him again."

"Is it possible she doesn't love him anymore?" Rose muses to herself, her finger tapping the dimple on her right cheek. "I don't think so. I've seen her heart line and I've read her cards. This seems like some kind of snafu."

"You know the cards aren't an exact science, Rose," I chastise her. Sometimes, it feels like I may be the only sane one among my two closest friends. They both treat their tarot practice as if it is the epitome of wisdom. I don't know how to explain that the cards are telling you what you want to hear. It's subjective, allowing you to read whatever you want in just any card. "I don't want to pull cards over this."

"Fine," she says. "I have a better idea anyway. Let's call her."

"You want me to call Petal up and tell her to meet us here so that we can talk her back into a relationship with her boyfriend?"

"Do you think it would be better if I called her?" Rose asks. "Maybe she wouldn't expect it coming from me. The element of surprise can be extremely effective."

She flips through her phone and dials Petal's number. While she waits for Petal to answer, she moves to the front door and flips the lock shut. The open sign flickers for a moment and then goes out as she pulls the cord. For good measure, she turns off the dim lights in the building so no one can see in, even if they pull into the parking lot. I guess the fact that this shop is going out of business has made Rose reprioritize Petal's relationship woes over her business.

"Petal," she greets her. "Let's get together for lunch."

I try to listen to what is being said on the other end of the line, but I'm having a hard time making out Petal's muffled voice. Rose could turn up the volume for me at least, so that I can more easily eavesdrop.

"Sure, let me get her for you." Rose walks across the room and hands me the phone.

"Petal, is everything okay?"

"Actually, I kind of need you to meet me at your apartment."

"Is it an emergency?"

"Well, I have to get the truck back to the store in an hour or I have to pay another hundred bucks. I don't think the cashier is going to let me flirt my way into a second discount." Her lilting laugh fills the other end of the line, but I can't shake the confusion dawning.

"Why do you have a truck and why is it at my apartment?"

Every word hits like a stone in my mouth as I slowly become aware of exactly what might be going on here. Petal has no intention of moving back in with Jason, nor is she in the frame of mind to find her own place. She thinks she's going to be crashing at *my* apartment.

Maybe I should say *our* apartment now.

"Essie, you know I had nowhere else to go."

"I'll be there in ten," I tell her, handing the phone back to Rose. I make my way to the back room and grab my bag. Rose grabs her keys when I emerge and I don't stop her. It might be best if we were both there so that I don't hurt Petal for the thoughtless way she announced she would be staying with me.

"I can be back up," Rose says with a shrug. "Maybe we can still have that intervention."

We leave the shop and she locks the door behind us. We ride in silence the whole way to my apartment. I'm so frustrated by Petal's cavalier attitude that we all have to go along with every single one of her plans. Rose also seems to be absorbed in thought, but I imagine her thoughts are a little less violent than mine are at the moment. Red and purple are the only colors I can see clearly which makes me wonder if Rose can read them in my aura. Maybe that's why she's so silent in the passenger seat.

When we pull into the apartment complex parking lot, Petal is sitting on the folded-down bed of the truck, her short legs swinging back and forth. Her pixie cut is pinned back with a yellow headband that matches her yellow shorts. She looks like a ray of sunshine, which is enough to make me feel furious.

"I think we need to talk about this," I call to her as I climb out of the driver's seat. Rose is still unfastening her seatbelt. She's in no hurry to dive between two sisters at odds with one another. "I don't exactly have room for another person in my apartment."

"You have the foldout sofa," Petal corrects with a smile. "I knew there was a reason I told you it was the practical choice. See how it's coming in handy now?"

"Was this your master plot all along? For me to buy the sleeper sofa so you had a place to crash when you impulsively break up with your boyfriend?"

"Well, no. But it does seem to have worked out in my favor. There's something to be said for trusting your intuition. I knew this couch would be right for your apartment."

I scoff at the idea of trusting her intuition to buy a couch. Even on my best days, I'm highly skeptical about the concept of intuition.

"Laugh all you want," Petal says. Her eyes are wide and open, a faint smile playing at the corners of her lips. "But I know exactly where I'm going to be sleeping tonight – and it's because I convinced you two years ago that *this* was the sofa you needed. Turns out, this was the sofa *I* needed."

"Then maybe you can reimburse me for it."

She tilts her head back and lets out another lilting laugh.

"I'm a bit strapped for cash, having made a large business investment recently," she says, the smile still fixed on her face. Her eyes crinkle at the corners. Despite this breakup and all of the associated turmoil on my end, she seems to be coping with these changes fairly well.

I grumble and walk past her to unlock the apartment. Petal follows me in with a cardboard box, and Rose brings another in directly on her heels. It looks like she has maybe fifteen boxes in the truck. I glance at the clock on the wall and realize time is ticking on Petal to get that truck back before she incurs the penalty fee. Truthfully, I'm glad she'll be leaving soon so that I have a minute alone to wrap my head around what just happened.

"The least you could do is grab a box, sis," Petal calls over her shoulder as she heads out to the car.

"I thought we were going to have an intervention," I hiss at Rose.

"Maybe this is what she needs, a little separation to gain clarity." Rose shrugs. "Looks like it's too late now to stop this. Where else would you have her go?"

I bite my tongue, knowing instinctively that Rose is right. Petal can't go back to her life in the townhome, and she has no other friends who are going to let her crash on their couch indefinitely. Rose has no room in her apartment for a guest, as cluttered as it is with plants and the more stereotypical crystal balls. I head outside and grab a box from the bed of the truck while Petal laughs.

"You could at least *pretend* not to be pissed at me," she says. "This could be good for us. Plus, it'll give us more time to plan your shop."

"Petal, I think we need to move your boxes in silently so that I don't say something I might regret later." I clench my jaw and drop the cardboard box on the living floor, letting it fall with a thud. It must be full of Petal's books from its weight and the *thunk* it makes when it hits the floor.

"She'll come around to it in time," Petal says to Rose who is heading back for another box. "The cards told me she would."

"You can read whatever you want in those cards," I grumble, but we keep carrying boxes into the apartment.

The only sound that escapes the three of us is the panting of our breath. None of us are what you might call "active" and lifting these overfilled boxes is more of a workout than we've had in the last six months. I can't believe Petal loaded up this truck all on her own. Then, it hits me: she probably didn't. Jason must have helped her which means he's *supporting* this whole crazy notion that they should break up. He probably knew last night she would be moving in here.

"I guess I should get the truck back," Petal says, grabbing her keys off the counter once we bring in the last box. "I'll be home in about a half hour, okay?"

"Don't start thinking of this as home. This is an *extremely* temporary arrangement."

"You're the best, Essie." Petal flashes me a smile that shows all of her teeth. She has them professionally whitened once a year. She climbs into the truck and carefully navigates out of the spot she parked in, directly in front of the building. Rose and I stand on the sidewalk and watch her go.

"I should go too," Rose says. "You two obviously have a lot you need to work out. Try not to be too hard on her. We don't know what's going on with her beneath the surface."

"Would you like me to read her palm and tell you what it says?" I know I shouldn't be short with Rose, but I can't help it. It feels like everyone around me is taking Petal's side and none of this makes sense.

"I know you don't believe in it, Esmerelda," she says. "But I think the least you can do is have a little grace for your sister. There's a part of her that is doing this for *you* just as much as you are doing this for *her*."

I swallow, knowing Rose is right. Petal has good intentions, even if they're a little off on the presentation.

"However, I *do* need a ride back to the store since we came here together," Rose says after giving me a beat.

"Right," I tell her. "Let's get moving. I want to be back when Petal gets here."

Petal and I would have all night to make sense of what was going on with her – and the day after that, and the day after that. Maybe all of this uninterrupted sister bonding could be used to help me figure out what's going on with her that brought about these massive changes all of a sudden. She's always been impulsive, but this is certainly a new standard for her. I know there has to be something more going on, and I'm determined to find out what it is.

Chapter 9

"**A**re you going to share that container of pad Thai or is it off-limits?" Petal asked, fork in the air as she reached for the cardboard takeout container in my hand. After the day we had, I could not bring myself to cook a meal for both of us, so we sprung for takeout. I pass her the container and a plate to serve herself.

"Are we going to talk about the elephant in the room?" I ask while she heaps rice noodles on her plate.

"And what elephant might that be?"

"How about the one where you made an executive decision to move in here without my knowledge or consent?" I pause for a moment. "Or, we could talk about the elephant of why you broke up with Jason when things were going so well."

"There were things you didn't know about," Petal says, eyes downcast.

"Whose fault is it that I didn't know? I would have taken your side, if you told me."

"I'm not blaming you, Essie. I'm just telling you that there's more to the story than what you see from the outside."

"And the reason you moved in with me instead of your own place is what exactly?"

Petal sighs and puts her fork down. For a moment, she closes her eyes and I watch her chest rise as she takes a deep breath that expands to her belly, a meditation technique she has been using since we took a one-time class four years ago. She says it helps clear her mind when she thinks about something difficult.

"First, I spent my extra money leasing that storefront."

"An endeavor that I did *not* encourage," I point out to her.

"It was an investment for *both* of us," Petal shrugs. "Not only did I not have any money, but I also just wanted to be close to you for a change. I'm going through a lot right now and you're my sister. Is that really so wrong?"

I feel my expression soften at this declaration of her love for me. Petal never has been demonstrative about her affection, even when she was little. A small statement like saying she wants to be close to me is just as good as if she declared her undying love. No matter what, we have a shared history. We have a story that transcends what we can find in relationships with men. For a moment, I think about Mark and the unceremonious way he sort-of dumped me. I have yet to hear a single word from him since then.

"I don't mind if you want to stay here for a *little while*," I emphasize the second half of my sentence. "But we also need to work on finding a place for you. You can't just sleep on my sofa for the rest of your life."

"Where am I going to find an apartment that doesn't require a security deposit? I really just need a few months to save up again."

"I happen to know an exceptional real estate agent who can probably find exactly what you want in an apartment—maybe even with no security deposit."

Her eyes grow round, lighting her up from within. I watch her process the fact that here I am, recommending Turner to find Petal a place to live, willingly inviting him into both of our lives.

"Are you going to stay on speaking terms with him again?"

"I don't see a way around it, so I guess you could say that."

"You looked so happy when you came to see me last night. Angry, but happy. I could tell there was a difference in you."

"There was no difference in me," I correct her quickly.

"Tell me about it."

"What is there to tell? We mostly talked about you and this misguided idea to open a shop. It seems to be a theme in our relationship."

"But there was still chemistry between you, yes?"

"What do you want me to say, Petal? That we made out outside the restaurant after four glasses of wine and decided to get back together?"

"If that happened, I would be over the moon for you."

I pause for a second and take in Petal's eager expression. Suddenly, it hits me that this store is *not* the only thing Petal has been up to behind the scenes. She chose her real estate agent with great care, even if she posed it as the most convenient option. I don't think she kept in touch with Turner after our breakup because she's a loyal sister. But now, this invasion of my privacy and the small interference in my love life strikes me as odd. Not only is she living with me right now, but she is meddling in places she has no business.

"You cooked up this whole scheme," I accuse her. "You thought you could strongarm me into opening a store and you picked Turner as the real estate agent because you wanted to see us get back together. And yet, you are so secretive with your own love life that I don't even know what the hell happened with Jason. And now, you're living on my sofa."

"It's all in the cards, Essie. Don't you see?"

"Please don't bring up tarot cards with me right now."

"I *have* to bring up the tarot cards. Don't you remember the reading I gave you? The pieces are all starting to click into place. When we asked the deck what was in store for your future, I got The Fool card which symbolizes new beginnings. You're on the cusp of a new chapter in your love life." She pauses and smiles. "Maybe I have the gift."

"It's hardly a gift," I scoff. "It's more like an elaborate ruse to con people out of their hard-earned money. There's no such thing as being able to read the future. Those cards are so subjective that you can read anything you want into them."

"Well, you might be a skeptic but *I'm* a true believer."

"Why don't we pull the cards for you right now then? We can find out where you should be living because I'm fairly certain the cards don't point to my living room sleeper sofa."

"Do you mean it?" Petal's face lights up at my offer. I should have known that my sarcastic response would trigger her delight. However, I'm so sure I can prove that you can read anything you want into these cards that I grab my bag and pull out the deck Petal made for me anyway.

"Shuffle the cards," I instruct her, watching as she cuts the deck and mixes the cards.

"Where should I live?" She directs her question at the deck as she transfers her own energy to the cards, customizing her reading specifically for her unique biochemistry. At least, that's what she tells herself. I'm ready to pull a card so I can put a spin on it that she needs to live somewhere other than here with me. She passes the deck over to me. I close my eyes, a holdout theatric of working for Rose.

The top card of the deck slides off and I flip it over, placing it on the table between us. *Page of Cups.*

"This card symbolizes a surprise," I begin, thinking as quickly as I can how to twist this card to mean something positive for me. "The Page of Cups means that you have a happy surprise coming soon. Joy is in the cards for you, along with a fresh start. I think it means you have a place to live on the horizon."

"I feel like you twisted that reading to match your own ends," Petal accuses me. "But still, I have to respect what the cards are saying. Maybe you're right. Maybe I should think about what it would look like to get my own apartment."

"Let's call Turner right now. See what he says about what we could find for you."

I pick up the phone and dial the number he called me from yesterday. I listen impatiently while the line rings, resisting the urge to give into my nervous habit of chewing on my nails. The last thing I want is for Petal to think I'm nervous about this phone call because I still have feelings for Turner. No, I'm nervous because I want my sister to move out of here; that's all there is to it.

When he picks up, we exchange greetings and I launch into the reason I'm calling him. I don't want him to think I'm calling him just to chat. Just because we had dinner together and had a good time doesn't mean we are friendly enough for phone calls. I put him on speaker so Petal doesn't get any ideas.

"What do you think? Can Petal find an apartment that doesn't require a security deposit?"

"We can certainly look. I can think of a couple properties that don't need a deposit, but I'm not sure if they'll be a good fit for Petal. The properties I can think of are a little roomy for someone living on their own unless she's thinking of bringing on a roommate."

"How roomy?" Petal asks.

"Two bedrooms – and you'll be paying for the additional space too, I might add."

"Two bedrooms would be perfect," Petal says.

"What in the world do you need two bedrooms for?" I ask her. "I was thinking you could find a nice loft space for a steal."

"I can use one as my studio. I might work on my art from home, but I need a good place to set up my things that isn't the dining room table." She shrugs. I know I won't talk her out of renting an apartment that's much bigger than she needs. Instead, I wonder if she has enough money to rent a bigger apartment without taking on a roommate but I keep my mouth shut.

"I'll put together a list of properties tomorrow," Turner says, ignoring the mounting tension and silence between Petal and me. "If you want one of them, you'll probably have to move quickly. Apartments in Charleston that don't need a security deposit tend to go quickly."

"Thanks, Turner," I tell him. We say goodbye and I hang up the line.

"Can we please talk about *your* elephant in the room?" Petal asks, a smile tugging at the corners of her mouth. "You still have feelings for Turner. It's written all over your face. You even have a *glow* about you after talking to him."

"I have a 'glow' because I'm excited to get you out of my apartment and into your own," I tell her, trying to make it sound like I'm teasing her even though there's a serious note behind the words. "This has nothing to do with Turner. Besides, even if it did, I would never rebound with an ex."

"I'm not sure it's considered rebounding if you were never in a relationship."

"Nice," I sarcastically respond. "Just what I wanted–a reminder that my relationship was one-sided. I think I'm going to call it a night."

"Don't go to bed angry," Petal frowns. "I didn't mean to upset you."

"I'm not angry." I sigh. "I'm just really tired, Petal. It's been an extremely long day and I want nothing more than to lay in bed and read a book."

"Do you mind if I take a bath? I love your clawfoot tub."

"Be my guest. There are bath bombs under the bathroom sink. Please don't use the pink ones because they stain the tub, but the purple ones smell heavenly."

Petal claps her hands and jumps up. I watch her rustle around in the many cardboard boxes lining the perimeter of my living room. She comes up with a pair of old sweatpants and a t-shirt she's had since high school.

"You won't even know I'm here," she promises, heading into the bathroom and shutting the door behind her.

"Towels are under the counter," I yell to her through the door. I hear the cabinet creak open as she looks for them.

As the water starts to run, I grab a stack of blankets from the hall closet and set up the sofa bed. We might be at odds right now, but I always take care of her. It's part of the reason I'm so upset she won't clue me into what's going on with her. How can I take care of her if I have no real idea what's happened? I toss the comforter over the thin mattress and survey my handiwork. My place looks like a hurricane hit and there is no spare room to walk around the couch. At least, not while it's pulled out in a bed like this with all the boxes surrounding it. We need to find another solution, but I know it won't happen tonight. Even Turner can't work magic that quickly.

Instead, I head to bed and dive beneath the covers. Tomorrow, I'm going to have to contend with everything going on: the new store, Petal's new apartment, closing Rose's shop, Turner. But at this precise moment, the only thing I can do is think of relaxing in bed with my eye mask and drifting off into peaceful slumber. I pull the blankets up over my head so I'm encased in darkness and let myself relax fully before finally slipping beneath the surface of consciousness and tumbling into a dream that reminds me of nothing in my real life whatsoever.

Chapter 10

By the time I get out of the shower and finish getting ready, Petal already has a fresh pot of coffee brewing – the good kind because she won't drink anything except locally roasted beans that have been put through her noisy coffee grinder. It was the whirring of the grinder that catapulted me out of bed. Today is my day off, but Petal couldn't let me sleep in even a little bit. I push down the irritation I feel at how she imposed on my life. I think she *meant* to be thoughtful, even if waking me up was a little thoughtless.

"Good morning, sunshine," she greets me when I wander into the kitchen. It was the same greeting our mom gave us every morning when we were growing up. She stopped greeting us like this when we were teens, surly in the morning until we had a cup of Folgers coffee. I never noticed when it gradually stopped, but it became a part of our shared lexicon, the vocabulary of our idyllic childhood.

"I was hoping yesterday was a dream," I tell her sarcastically as I pour a generous cup of her coffee and lighten it with half and half. She already has it sitting out on the counter, waiting for me. I have to admit, this isn't the worst way to wake up in the morning. It's been a while since I had someone make me a cup of coffee.

"Today is your day off," Petal says, changing tacks without acknowledging my barb. She must have already had a cup of coffee or two based on her perkiness. "I was thinking we could do something together today."

I sigh. It isn't like I have any other leads on things to do today. Even if we stay right here in the apartment, Petal will just be underfoot because she literally lives in my living room now. I can't think of anything I want to do less than spend an afternoon in my living room, crowded with all of Petal's worldly belongings. Ideally, we would hunt for her new apartment, but I don't think that's in the cards for us yet.

"I thought we could spend the day at the shop."

"Petal, I spend five days a week at the shop. I don't want to hang out there on my day off."

"Not with Rose," she corrects. "*Your* shop."

"You're choosing to spend the day at that creepy shop?"

"You agreed that you were going to give this thing a shot." Petal sets her coffee mug down on the counter and puts her hands on her hips. "How are you going to give it a real shot if we never get the place in working order? We need to make a plan."

This is the first time in my entire life that Petal has asked *me* to make a plan. It makes me pay more attention to her, appraising her. She looks just as put together as she always does, as if she spent the night sleeping on a king-sized mattress with Egyptian cotton sheets instead of old, scratchy flannel on a fold-out couch. She has a notebook out on the counter in front of her. A quick glance tells me she has been making a list.

"I find this extremely rich coming from you," I finally tell her. "You haven't had a plan at all this week, and now you're trying to bully me into making one with you?"

"I did have a plan, and I'm following it."

"Your plan was to move in with me without giving me any advance notice?"

"Okay, maybe not all parts of the plan were ideal. But that doesn't mean I didn't have one."

"Wouldn't you rather look for an apartment instead of thinking about that creepy place?"

Petal shakes her head no and clicks the top of her pen. She heads to the living room and starts to rummage around in her boxes until she comes back with her sneakers.

"Let's go," she commands. "You can take the coffee to go."

With a sigh, I realize she is going to dig her heels in so I pour my coffee into a travel mug and slip on my own sneakers. At least I'm already dressed in my gym shorts and an old t-shirt to spend the day in that dusty storefront. Petal prattles on while we drive to the outskirts of the downtown sprawl. Most of the time, I tune her out as she talks about all of the changes she wants to make. The only conversation I'm interested in having with her is one where she searches for a place to live.

"Oh, I almost forgot. I made you your own key to the store," she says, digging through her cavernous handbag. She presents me with a turquoise key, my favorite color, and I soften a little bit at the small gesture. I hand Petal my key ring for her to slip it on alongside my apartment key and the key to Rose's shop.

"Thank you," I tell her, trying to sound sincere.

"You'll be thanking me once we get this place up and running for real."

I flip on my blinker and we navigate over the concrete sidewalk and into the parking lot. I try to avoid the massive potholes and park in the open space directly in front of the empty store. It still has a rental advertisement in the front window, its red lettering faded with its exposure to the noonday sun. I take my turquoise key back from Petal and slip it into the lock.

"I have a vision for this space." Petal walks around me and into the center of the room. I fumble along the wall for the light switch. The overhead fluorescent lighting doesn't do much to make this place feel more inviting. "Picture it: lavender paint on the walls, the velvet chairs from Rose, these reclaimed wooden tables. We can make it look a little more visually interesting by dividing the space up with gauzy curtains suspended from the ceiling."

Petal strides through the space, pointing out where she would hang the curtains, where the accent wall will go, and where the cash register fits into the room without interrupting the "flow" of the space. She must say "flow" at least ten times in the span of her five-minute diatribe.

"Maybe we should just start by cleaning this place," I volunteer. While I know Petal does have a good eye for interior design, I'm a little hesitant to jump full force into her ideas.

"Cleaning is a good first step," she agrees. I'm a little surprised at how she takes to it. Petal is usually five to ten steps ahead of everyone else and hates backward movement. She must have some inkling of how dirty this place is if she's agreeing to put a halt to her plans for painting and refurbishing this place to clean it. It's decidedly unglamorous to scrub the floors and clear out the dust, but she doesn't hesitate. "Give me your keys and I'll run to the store to pick up some cleaners."

"And leave me here in this dust factory?"

"You need time to get to know the space before we start redecorating."

"I disagree," I say. "In fact, I think that I could use to know *less* about this space."

"You're staying and I'll be right back."

Reluctantly, I toss her the keys to my car and send up a little prayer that she won't total it on the way to the store two blocks over. She smiles and waves before leaving.

As soon as she's gone, I look for something I can use as a doorstop to prop open the front door and start to air out the space so that I don't have to keep breathing in all of this dust. Instead, dust swirls in the air as the outdoor breeze rushes in, making me sneeze. Very patiently, I try to spend my time in the space seeing it the way Petal does. I look beyond the mannequins and the thick layer of grime that coats everything, but it isn't the easiest thing in the world. I start to get the sense that there are indeed good bones to the space under it all.

The main room is huge and open with tall ceilings that make it feel bigger than it really is. I walk the perimeter of the shop and realize what a small footprint it has. Petal must have gotten a great deal on this place because it's far too small for most businesses. That must be why it sat vacant. Fortunately, all we need here are a couple of tables and a cash register. I don't love the white and black ceiling tiles above me, but I know that most clients will never look up to see them, not with all the changes Petal intends to make.

I start to make my own plans for what the space needs: some mood lighting instead of the harsh fluorescents and a few extra chairs for waiting clients. When I think about this place being filled with customers, I laugh aloud. Rose never has people waiting for their turn in the hot seat; what makes me think this shop will need a waiting area?

"I'd love to hear what's so funny."

A small shock runs through me and I glance around quickly. My only exit is blocked by a man and I have no idea how long Petal is going to be at the store. She left twenty minutes ago already. *Why* did I have to leave the front door open? It was like I left an invitation for some weirdo from the bar down the strip to come right on in.

"Petal told me you'd be here," he says. *Petal.* The man knows Petal, so it must be okay. I take a step closer to make out his facial features. With his back against the sun, it's hard to identify anyone in particular. "Plus, I needed to reclaim my sign."

"Turner," I breathe a sigh of relief.

"This is a great space," he says, looking around. "Petal knew exactly what she was looking for. It was like she manifested the ideal place for you."

"Knowing her, she probably *did* manifest it. It's one of her hobbies, but I believe she refers to it as a lifestyle."

"What are you going to do with the space?"

I give him a quick rundown of what Petal thought would work best combined with my own appraisal of the space. Together, we walk around the small room and try to envision a bright future in this dank space. Every time I make a revolution around the room, it becomes clearer to me that this is the perfect space. It just needs a little bit of elbow grease to really shine.

"But I think we should start with just cleaning it up," I finish as we arrive back at the front door.

"When you need to paint, give me a call. A tall, strong man like me can make quick work of these walls." I'm not sure, but I think Turner actually winks at me.

We haven't spoken in two years and now he acts as if we've been friends all along.

"Turner." I take a deep breath. "I know we have a history and I really appreciate you being there for Petal. But I think we should keep this purely professional."

"I wasn't suggesting that we get naked and go skinny dipping in the river, Ess. I was offering to help you paint because I am significantly taller than both you and Petal. In case you haven't noticed, these ceilings are quite high."

"Are you sure it's just about the paint?"

"Well, I have to admit I feel a little responsible in this situation. I let Petal lease it on your behalf, knowing you would never agree to this plan. The least I can do is make it presentable for you with a fresh coat of paint."

"I'll let you know if we need a hand." I don't want to look a gift horse in the mouth. The truth is Petal and I would struggle to paint this place. "But first, I need to know if you have any leads on apartments for Petal. Somehow, she came to the idea that staying at my place was the best option."

"I heard that," Petal says from the doorway, bags of cleaning supplies looped over her arms.

"Maybe you were meant to overhear. You know what they say about eavesdroppers."

"I know what they say about sisters who would turn their own flesh and blood out on the street when they have a perfectly comfortable sleeper sofa in their living room."

"I don't have any leads just yet, but I'll let you know as soon as I come across one," Turner promises. "I'll give you a call later. I have to get back with this sign. Real estate doesn't sell itself."

Petal waits until he's securely back in his car before turning to me with a little smile playing at the corners of her mouth.

"*I'll call you later,*" she mocks. "You two are definitely going to get back together."

"We are most definitely *not* going to get back together, so you can stop that idea right in its tracks." I redirect her attention back to the task. "Did you get everything we need at the store? I think we should get moving ASAP if we want to be out of here by dark – and I most definitely do not want to be in this part of town after the sun sets."

"Did you *see* the way he looks at you, Essie?"

"He looks at me like I'm the sucker who just leased his least desirable property."

"Whatever you say," she shrugs. "Let's get cleaning."

Chapter 11

Three hours later, I have to admit this place looks pretty good. Petal may be a little spontaneous when it comes to a lot of things, but she is a fantastic cleaner. If her art career doesn't pan out, she would make an excellent maid. She could even run her own business cleaning houses for people; she's *that* good at making the dirtiest places sparkle when she's finished with them. Not only did she help me dust and wipe down every surface, but she dusted the walls while I scrubbed the floor. When she pulled away the dirty cleaning pads, I had to admit she was right to wipe down literally every surface in here.

"Let's go to the home improvement store." We're sitting on the floor of the fresh space, drinking the sodas we purchased from the Mexican restaurant on the strip.

"Can't you be happy with the progress we made today?" I ask her. "Let's save the painting for another time."

"We need to get this place up and running. Rose is shutting her place down in two weeks, remember?"

"It doesn't *need* to be running by the time she shuts down. We can take our time and chip away at it."

"Essie," Petal chides me. "Two days have gone by already and we haven't done anything more than clean up. You need to kick it into high gear if we're going to get this place running."

"I'll tell you what," I say. "How about I drop you off at the home improvement store and I head home to make dinner?"

"Don't you want to pick out paint samples with me?" Her expression is crestfallen.

"You have a great vision for this place. I trust your design judgment." This seems to appease her. "Why don't you design the place and surprise me with it in a few weeks? I still have to help Rose out at the shop, reading for clients and breaking things down so we can be out in two weeks. Divide and conquer, just like the old days."

Petal brightens up at the prospect of taking this project on all by herself.

"Are you sure you trust me to do this?"

"Of course," I tell her, realizing as I say it that I honestly do. "You have great artistic vision. I think you'll know exactly what to do to get this place shipshape."

"I'll need some help painting," she muses.

"I almost forgot. Turner volunteered to help paint. Give him a call when you're ready."

"I think he volunteered to help *you* paint," she corrects. "But I'll try to enlist him."

Petal stands up and grabs her purse. We're both grimy and sweaty after spending so many hours getting this place in working order. I can't wait to go home and take a scalding shower. I plan to hit it first, before I start dinner for the two of us.

"I'm ravenous," Petal announces as we walk back to the car. "What's on the menu for dinner?"

"Black bean burgers." It's the only food I have in the freezer that isn't a single-serve meal. I wasn't exactly planning for extended company and I hardly ever cook a full meal just for myself. The leftovers never seem to disappear and I hate throwing food away. If Petal doesn't want to eat some freezer-burned black bean burgers with me, she can find her own meal. "Are you going to be okay to walk the three blocks home from the home improvement store?"

"I *think* I can manage," she says, sniffing. "Are you sure you don't want to go in with me?"

"If you want a black bean burger when you get home, I need to throw them on the skillet."

"Fair enough," she says and turns the music up louder. I let the volume ride until I pull up to the home improvement store and she leaves. Then, I turn it back down to a lower decibel and switch it to instrumental music that feels more soothing.

When my phone rings as I'm pulling away from the curb, I don't even check the screen to see who it is.

"What do you want, Petal?" I growl into the phone. "I literally just pulled away from the curb."

I'm met with silence on the other end of the phone and then throat-clearing. Not Petal, a man's voice. I pull the phone away from my ear and look at the name that flashes across the caller ID on the screen: *Mark.*

"Oh, sorry. I really thought you were my sister," I apologize, but what I really want to know is why he's calling me now. I thought he made his point pretty clear a few days ago that we were through. He doesn't volunteer any information, so I ask what I can do for him.

"I was wondering if you wanted to go out for drinks with me."

"Did we not have the same conversation a few days ago about how I might 'get the wrong idea?'" I try to make my use of air quotes obvious over the phone.

"Esmerelda, I didn't mean that we should stop seeing each other. I just meant that we never had any discussions about being exclusive."

"And let me get this straight: you want to see other people, but you would also like to see me on occasion when your other plans fall through."

"You're twisting my words."

"Fine," I tell him. "Drinks in two hours?"

"I'll meet you at our usual spot," he says before hanging up.

I find myself trying to silence a small part in the back of my brain that tells me Mark wasn't meant for me because there's someone else out there. I think about Petal's comment about Turner and his feelings for me before I shake the thought loose and go inside. I toss the black bean burgers in the microwave to defrost and turn on the shower to get the hot water flowing. The only person who truly seems to understand me right now is Turner. Like my knight in shining armor, he helped Petal find a place for me to work, volunteered to help her get it opening-day ready, and is looking for an apartment she can afford. It sounds like he's doing a lot for Petal, but I wonder if he's doing it all for *me*.

As I spend twenty minutes in the shower, I think through our conversations. The banter is quick and easy despite our time apart, but I honestly have no idea what's going on in his life right now. Is his sister married? Are his parents still alive? Does he have a girlfriend?

It's this last one that strikes me the hardest. I feel it viscerally in the pit of my belly. He had every right to move on with his life. Our past is strictly in the past, and we called it quits because I couldn't commit to a lifetime with him when Petal required so much of me. Maybe this is the parallel I see now: Petal needed someone to help her and Turner was there for her. Was this meant to send me a message about his availability, his understanding that I ended things with him in the past because Petal needed me more?

I resolve not to think about it as I turn the water off. Petal will be able to smell it on me if she thinks I'm even contemplating the possibility of a future with Turner. Meanwhile, I have a date with Mark—if you can call it a date. I dry off, dress in my most comfortable jeans, and pad to the kitchen to start frying up some burgers. As soon as I get them on the skillet and start to hear them sizzle, Petal comes in the front door with a handful of paint chips.

"I couldn't decide on just one," she says, revealing the array of colors she's selected. There are sage greens and dreamy lavenders, deep navy blues and charcoal greys. "I need to take them to the shop and see them with the natural light in there."

"I'm sure you'll make the right decision," I tell her. "You have an eye for color."

She glows under my praise.

"I can't wait until you see what I have in store for you," she crows.

"I hope it's nothing too extravagant. It's better to get this place open than to get bogged down in these silly design elements." I want to warn her that we won't be able to cover the cost of this apartment and a security deposit on her new apartment without getting a few clients through the door in the early days. Two weeks left on my paying gig before we have to make it on our own.

"Go ahead and tell everyone you're opening the doors next Friday," she promises. "Turner already agreed to help me, though he seemed disappointed you weren't going to be there."

"You got us into this mess; you deal with the marketing and the grand opening." I flip the burgers in the pan and pull lettuce out to wrap them in. Petal grabs a bottle of barbecue sauce.

"Don't worry about a thing," she says. "All you have to do is focus on your intuition. People are going to be able to tell if you aren't giving it an honest effort."

"I've been doing this for *years*," I remind her. "I know how to fake a tarot card reading."

"I wish you wouldn't say things like that. You never know who might overhear you."

"We're the only people here, and it's honestly how I feel. Tarot cards don't mean a thing, no matter who pulls them."

"Haven't you realized that the reading I gave you the other day is *already* coming true?"

"You told me I was going to have major upheaval in my life: I lost my job and somehow got roped into starting a new shop with you. The cards also said I was going to have a spark in my love life. I guess I should go ahead and tell you that I'm meeting Mark for drinks tonight."

"The whole reading is true," Petal says mysteriously. "Even if *you* can't see it yet."

"Do you know something I don't?"

"Don't I always?" Petal tilts her head back and laughs. "It's the joy of being the little sister. I see things more clearly than you do."

"Maybe you should be the psychic," I grumble. "That would make more sense for this little adventure you have planned for us."

"Esmerelda Jane Milos," she says, shaking her head. The only person who called me that was our mom. Petal rarely uses my full name, only when she really wants to drive a point home. "I have planned this entire adventure for *both* of us. I can't wait until you fully understand what's going on here. I hope then you'll have a little more enthusiasm."

"And when, exactly, do you think you'll enlighten me as to what's going on here?"

"As soon as it makes sense."

"Ah, yes. I understand now." I roll my eyes as I flip the burgers onto each of our waiting plates. Petal pours a swirl of sauce on hers first, then mine. We wrap them in the huge butter lettuce leaves and sit down at the bar in the kitchen where we always eat when we're together here. Even if we wanted to eat in front of the TV, it's off-limits now that Petal lives there.

"Esmerelda, there are simply some things going on that are too perfect for you to embrace just yet. But I've seen it in your cards. You're going to come around to all of these changes, even if it takes us a few months to get there."

"And if it takes longer than a few months for me to come around?"

"It won't."

"I guess we'll have to agree to disagree."

I take a big bite of my burger and Petal does the same, chewing thoughtfully as she gazes at me. I notice just how much she's aged in recent years, the crinkles around her eyes looking just a little more pronounced than they used to – a sign that she's laughed and smiled a lot in her twenty-seven years. She's gotten a little softer around the middle, but not by much. If I hadn't spent so much time with her when mom died, I'm not sure I would have even noticed the extra five or ten pounds she's put on. It's subtle on her small frame. She catches me appraising her and smiles.

"Maybe we should read the cards tonight before you leave for your date," she says. "You know, it's part of my bedtime ritual."

"There are a million other things I would prefer to do tonight."

"Suit yourself. I'll still pull a spread for you and tell you about it in the morning."

I finish my burger just as Petal takes the last bite of hers. I stack our plates on top of each other and leave them by the kitchen sink. I start to tidy up the kitchen while Petal watches before she shuffles back into the living room. I hear her break into one of her cardboard boxes and come back to the table with her sketchbook and watercolor paints.

"Do you mind if I set up shop at your dining room table?"

"Be my guest," I tell her. "Actually, I take that back. Maybe I *shouldn't* ask you to be my guest. You might get the wrong idea and move in with me."

"Ha," she laughs, sarcastically. "You're the best sister in the whole wide world, you know that?"

"Trying to butter me up so that I invite you to sleep in the bed with me instead of on the sofa?"

"Is it working?"

"Not a chance," I tell her, but I catch myself smiling. Things with Petal seem to be easy in a way that we've never really had before. In some ways, she's moved ahead with her adult life and doesn't require any intervention from me anymore. At other times, I wonder how she managed this far into her adult life on her own – like when she showed up on my doorstep and announced she was moving in. I resolve to help her make her own decisions about her life and stop enabling her to crash into my life starting tomorrow.

Until then, I need to get ready for this date. I swipe on some mascara, tie my hair into a better topknot, and slip on a pair of flats rather than heels. I'm too tired from cleaning all day to bother dressing up for something as casual as this promises to be.

"I'm headed out," I call to Petal, hunched over the dining room table with her brush and a pad of thick watercolor paper.

"Have fun," she says suggestively. "But remember that you have a roommate now."

"Classy," I tell her, shutting the front door behind me. I drive ten blocks over to the bar where we had our first date, the one where we met after we both swiped right on the app. We have been coming here often ever since. Now, I wonder if this is where Mark picks up all of his lovers, how many women he actually seduced here at this bar. Maybe everyone is on it except me.

I climb out of the car and enter into the thick smoke of the bar. The lighting is dim, better to blur the rough edges on the men and women who come here. I sidle up to the bar and scan the faces upturned toward the baseball game on the televisions behind the counter. Then, I see him.

"You actually came," Mark says when I slide onto the barstool next to him at Finnegan's. "I wasn't sure you would after how we left things last time."

"Admittedly, I have a lot going on right now, and it just felt like I needed to get out of my life for a few hours," I say. "This was the best offer I had."

Mark places one of his warm hands over mine on the bar and signals to the bartender with his other. He orders me a Long Island iced tea and another round of Jack and Coke for himself. I wonder how many rounds he's already had while waiting for me here. I wonder how many of the girls sitting around us have given him his number, how many of them think I'm stupid for sitting here with a man who doesn't believe in serial monogamy—at least, not with me.

"Tell me what's been going on," he offers when the bartender slides the tall glass in front of me.

I launch into a detailed explanation of how Petal threw all of this on me, the storefront, and our new living arrangement. I conveniently leave out the details about Turner.

"But you didn't invite me out to hear about my problems," I finish.

"So your sister is sleeping on your couch?"

"My whole living room is stacked high with her boxes."

He grunts a little bit and stirs his drink. I take a long sip of iced tea to fill the silence, stirring the ice in the cup with the straw.

"Maybe this was a mistake," he says. "I thought maybe we could spend a little time together but your sister is staying with you."

Suddenly, it all becomes clear to me.

"You thought this was a booty call," I say, my voice rising. "You invited me here to liquor me up and then you wanted to come back to my place. Why can't we ever go to *your* place?"

"Because I think that might—"

"Give me the wrong idea," I finish for him. "Yeah, I see where this is headed. You pick up the tab. I'm going home."

I slide off the barstool and pivot on my heel, grateful for the flats. The Long Island iced tea was stronger than I was used to, and I was already feeling its effects. It wouldn't have been a very dramatic exit had I finished the drink and had to stumble off in my heels. How could I have let myself think that this was a good idea?

I sit in my car and rest my forehead on the top of the wheel, letting out a frustrated scream. I should have known that this thing with Mark was never going to go anywhere. He had made it excruciatingly clear that we didn't mean anything to one another. Like a fool, I had come here and tried to resurrect something dead in the water. I wanted to tell someone about what this was like, but the only person I could think to tell was Turner.

This can't be a good sign.

Chapter 12

Rose and I are sitting in companionable silence at her shop, watching through the windows as the rain comes down. We just finished boxing up some of the more fragile items we have in here as decoration: the crystal ball we never use, the crystals that project rainbows around the shop, the picture frames that used to adorn the walls. The place looks like we're going out of business and we still have a week left to take clients.

"Are you sure you want to do this?"

"Essie, there's no way we can keep on doing this with the rent at its new price. Besides, I have a new job lined up, remember?" She pauses for a minute and fiddles with the packing tape on the table in front of her. "And so do you."

"Please tell me you aren't upset that Petal did this," I say. "I know you could have opened another storefront in a different location if Petal hadn't introduced competition into the market. If it bothers you, maybe we could transfer the lease to your name."

Part of me is desperately hoping Rose will say that she minds so I can get out of this entire mess. Petal has come home every day this week covered in paint, thoroughly exhausted. She passes out on the sofa bed around 8:00 each night, an accomplishment for a self-proclaimed night owl. If she knew Rose was against her opening this shop, maybe she would be willing to allow Rose to reimburse her for the expense of the lease. I would be home free, would still have a steady job, *and* I wouldn't have to work with my sister.

"I'm *glad* you're doing this," Rose interrupts my reverie. "I don't want the responsibility of running the store anymore, but I love what I do. It's the perfect way for me to read fortunes for people without having to deal with the financials."

"Hold that thought," I tell her as my phone starts to buzz in my back pocket.

"I think I found a couple of apartments that would work great for Petal." I wish I had looked at the caller ID before answering. Turner. We haven't spoken since he offered to help paint, but I have a feeling he's been down helping Petal. She claims to be almost ready for the big reveal, and I highly doubt she could have pulled this off all on her own. I blush a little at the thought I had to call him and tell him about my non-breakup the other night. Truthfully, I was grateful that I hadn't let my itching fingers press his number. Part of wished I was at the store with him and Petal, making up for lost time. The other part of me told me that he was no good for me, that this certainly wans't the new beginning Petal had read in my cards.

"Can we go look at them tomorrow?" I ask, already seeing a day off slip through my fingers yet again.

"We need to go today," he says. "These apartments are going like hotcakes. If you want your sister off your sofa, you'll drop everything and meet me there in an hour."

I sigh and agree to meet him. It isn't exactly like Rose and I are bombarded with people at the moment, and I know she would tell me to go. Still, I hesitate because I know our time in this place is limited. When we work together in the future, the dynamic will be shifted, forever altered. I want to preserve this time as best I can.

"You're leaving me," Rose announces when I get off the phone. Her lower lip sticks out in a pout.

"Just for a little bit. Turner found some apartments for Petal to look at. He's convinced that if we don't meet right now to go look at them, they'll be gone before we even have a chance."

"Turner." Rose pauses and closes her eyes. "Could this be love for Esmerelda?"

"He's a real estate agent, Rose. We aren't hopping into bed together."

"I can see a future here," she says, taking on that mysterious tone of voice she uses with all of our customers. She opens her eyes and flashes me a smile. "Get out of here and go get Petal off your couch."

I grab my things and race to the car, calling Petal on the way. She agrees to meet me at the new shop, allowing us to ride together. Part of me is hoping for a sneak peek of the inside of the store. I hope Petal has gotten rid of the mannequins instead of dressing them up and using them as part of the décor. When I pull up in front of the shop, she's sitting outside on the curb.

"I don't get to look inside?" I ask, realizing just how disappointed I am.

"Tomorrow." She smiles triumphantly. "I'm nearly finished but I need a second set of hands to put on the finishing touches. That's where you come in."

"I guess I can help tomorrow." Again, I see my day off disappearing. There won't be any luxurious mornings or pancake breakfasts soon. I'll be lucky to even get a cup of coffee to go. Petal has been up and out the door by eight every morning this week. "Right now, I think we should focus on this apartment hunt."

"Is it so bad sharing an apartment with me, sis?"

I take my eyes away from the road and throw her a look that answers the question for both of us. She laughs and it sounds like a bell ringing.

"I'll have an open mind about these apartments, but you know I'm strapped for cash at the moment. If they require a security deposit or first and last month's rent, then I'm officially out of the running for them."

"I have some savings I can chip in to help you out if one of these apartments is perfect. It might not be enough for the first and last month's rent, but maybe it would cover a small security deposit." I start to tally up the thousand dollars I have in the bank. I'm hesitant to let it go, not knowing what my income will look like when we open this shop. Is it worth it to get Petal off my sofa? We're going to need a little professional distance if we'll also be working together.

We pull up in front of a tall brick building, ivy covering one side of the façade. It looks like it holds three or four floors of apartments with clean glass windows spaced evenly along its front. Despite the aged appearance of the exterior, you can tell from the condition of the glass, the freshly painted front door, and the landscaping outside that this building has been meticulously maintained and brought into this century. Turner is waiting for us on the stoop outside.

"What do you think?" He is smiling from ear to ear. "It's a beautiful building right in the heart of downtown. It'll be close to work, close to shopping."

"Let's see the inside before we get ahead of ourselves," Petal volunteers. I wonder when she became so diplomatic. In the past, she would have swooned over the way this building looked from the outside, almost making her decision before we ever saw the interior.

Turner opens the front door for us and we walk through the well-lit hallways until we get to the stairwell. He starts up it and takes us to the third floor. I notice Petal is panting behind me as she climbs the stairs. I hope this climb isn't going to be the thing that takes this apartment off the table.

"Welcome to your new apartment," Turner says, opening the door on unit 302. His bravado must make him a great real estate agent.

Petal walks slowly into the apartment, trailing along the perimeter of the main living areas. The kitchen, breakfast nook, and living room are all one large, open room. She walks slowly and purposefully around the edges, running her hand along the countertops, the windowsills, the chair railing. The sunlight bounces through the window and reflects off the glossy wood floors. I almost lose my breath; this place is that beautiful.

"It's the perfect place for you, Petal," I volunteer when she hasn't said anything. I'm not sure if I really mean it, but I'm desperate to convince her that this is the right move. "This natural light would be perfect for your painting."

"It *is* beautiful," she says thoughtfully, moving further into the apartment. She pokes her head into the bathroom. "No clawfoot tub, though."

"I hardly think you can make that a criterion for renting an apartment."

"*You* have a clawfoot tub," she corrects me.

"I'm lucky." I turn to Turner. "Can you please tell my sister that she'll never find a place to live if she sets ridiculous wish lists like this?'

"I hate to say it, Petal," he says with a shrug. "Your sister is right. If you want a place that has no security deposit *and* a clawfoot tub, the odds of finding something that will work for you is extremely slim."

"I guess I can live without the tub."

She makes her way past the bathroom to the last door on the right. She opens it and then comes right back out, obviously disappointed.

"Turner, this place only has one bedroom."

"I know you wanted two so that you could have a studio space, but the lighting in here is so perfect that I thought you might not mind setting up your studio in the living room. It's spacious and has room for an easel right over here." Turner walks to the edge of the living room, right next to the windows. "You'd still have room for a couch and entertainment center here. It would be a little crowded, but picture what it would be like to paint in front of these windows."

Petal bites her bottom lip.

"I need two bedrooms."

"Petal, listen to Turner. This place is perfect for you and it doesn't require a security deposit. I know you're used to having a studio at Jason's btu this place is good enough."

"You don't understand," Petal says, turning to me slowly. "I *need* two bedrooms."

"In your price range, that's going to be pretty difficult," Turner pipes in. "I would caution you to reconsider that."

"This isn't how I wanted to tell you," Petal says, tears glittering her eyes.

"Tell me *what*?" My heart starts racing. If Petal has been keeping a secret from me, then there must be something seriously wrong. I wonder if this secret has anything to do with the end of her relationship with Jason. Sweat starts to break out on the back of my neck the longer she goes without speaking.

"I need a second bedroom because I'm pregnant."

It sounds like a rush of wind is engulfing me and I suddenly need to sit down for a minute. There is *no* way that Petal can be pregnant and yet, I see the signs. Her immediate craving for blueberry pancakes at Jestine's, the extra weight she's carrying around the middle, the exhaustion that leaves her collapsing on the sofa bed every night. I'm sitting on the floor with my back pressed up against the white cabinetry when Petal comes over and sits down next to me.

"How can that be true?" I finally manage to ask.

"Well, I think you know the basics," Petal tries to joke, but it falls flat.

"But you and Jason are broken up. Why would you leave him when you're pregnant?"

"I left *because* I'm pregnant," she says. "I always knew he didn't want kids, but it became clear when I found out I was pregnant. He wanted me to have an abortion. I couldn't imagine doing that to this little life inside me." She places one hand over the small swelling in her stomach.

"Should I leave you two alone for a minute?" Turner asks. He stands awkwardly apart from us in the corner. He's never been good with heavy emotional moments, and he doesn't have a clear role in this scenario.

"No, you can stay," Petal says, with a wave of her hand. "I think we're almost done here."

"The cards," I suddenly gasp and Petal nods.

"I told you they were accurate. New life."

"I hate to interrupt this conversation, but we really need to leave now," Turner says. "This apartment is extremely popular and we only had a twenty-minute window for our viewing before the next people come through."

Petal and I stand up from our place on the floor, and she takes my hand in hers.

"Promise me you aren't mad at me for this?"

"Petal, why would I be *mad* at you for being pregnant?"

"This isn't the way you wanted my life to go," she says. "You always wanted me to do it the right way: stable career, then marriage, *then* kids. Now, I have a painting career, a fortunetelling shop, and no boyfriend to round things out. I don't expect you to let me live on your sofa indefinitely, but I *need* a two-bedroom apartment for the nursery."

"Well, I have bad news on that front," Turner interjects. "All of the apartments I booked us to look at today are only one bedroom. I didn't know that a second bedroom was a strict rule for the lease. I thought budget was the more important issue."

"It's okay, Turner," I tell him. "We can regroup later in the week with another set of listings. I think we all need a little time to process."

We make our way out of the apartment building and stand awkwardly on the sidewalk. The three of us must make an odd picture. Petal and I are still holding hands and Turner stands there, on the outskirts of our sister relationship as he has always been. I'm sure this strikes him as a repeat of the last time he and I were together. It's always been Petal and me against the world – and now, we have a new life to shepherd into existence.

"I don't know if I can find a two-bedroom apartment in your budget," he confesses. "I'm a good real estate agent, but I'm not a magician."

"Keep your eyes open," I tell him. "We can wait for a little while."

I suddenly feel a rush of affection for my little sister. For the first time in a week, I don't mind her crashing on my couch. She trusts me enough to move in with me, to allow me to walk with her through this pregnancy. While I wish she had found a better time and a better way to tell me, I can't imagine her being apart from me with this new life on the way. She doesn't need to be alone with this, and I can't believe that Jason would have allowed her to leave knowing she was going to have his baby. Even if he didn't want kids, I didn't think he could be so callous.

Petal and I climb back into my car, but I don't make any move to put it in gear. I'm turning over an idea in my mind and I need to let it percolate. We sit there in the silence of the car, the only sound the rushing of other cars coming perilously close to us on these crowded streets. Finally, I can see my way around the mountainous problem in front of me.

"Let's move in together," I say.

"We've *already* moved in together," Petal corrects me. "And you hate it."

"I hate that you're living on my sofa, in the middle of my living room, surrounded by a mountain of cardboard boxes. And I don't mean that you should move into my apartment, per se. I was thinking more about us getting a new apartment for *both* of us – all three of us."

"You want to live with me and a baby?"

"I can't let you do this entirely on your own," I tell her. "If Jason doesn't want to step up and be a man, then he is going to be the one who misses out. I know this baby is going to be something special because it's a part of *you*. You're going to need help. Being a single mom isn't easy. Wouldn't it make the most sense if we just moved in together?"

"But we're already working together. You'll need some space."

"We can stagger our shifts at the store, choose different days off like Rose and I do now. Besides, I think you'll probably spend most of your time in the office painting while we do the readings up front."

"What about when you want to bring a boyfriend home?"

"My love life isn't exactly going places at the moment," I laugh. "My last boyfriend still wants to see me, but only if we sleep together. Do you really think it'll be a problem for me to not bring a random guy home?"

"But we would need a three-bedroom apartment."

"Well, with your budget and mine combined, we could probably afford a three-bedroom."

Petal stops to mull this over as she gazes out the passenger window back at the brick façade of the building we just left. A trio of people enter through the door, and I wonder if they are there to view the same apartment we just left.

"Can I think about it?" she asks.

Her response surprises me. Since when does she need to think over the best option she's been given? I'm offering her a place to live that she can afford, built-in help for those nighttime feedings, *and* she gets the joy of living with me. It sounds like a match made in heaven – if anything, *I'm* the one who needs to think it over.

"Of course," I say, not wanting to reveal the hurt in my voice. I start the car and put it in drive, navigating away from the apartment building and back toward the shop. We ride in silence the whole way there, but it doesn't feel uncomfortable. I wonder what Petal's thinking, but I know enough not to ask. She'll let me know when she's ready.

"Do you want to come in and see the progress?" Petal asks when I pull into the parking lot.

"You told me I could see it tomorrow."

"I'm offering to let you see it right now," she says. "Because the truth is I need help to put the finishing touches on it, and I don't think Turner is going to come back and help me after I just dropped the baby bomb on him."

"I bet he would come back and help you *because* you're pregnant," I correct her. "He's nothing if not chivalrous."

"Still, I'd prefer not to put him through that. I just need someone to help me hold the ladder. Actually, it would be better if *you* could climb the ladder and I could hold it steady for you." She rubs her belly. "I don't know if I'm supposed to be climbing ladders in my condition."

I look at her and see the small mischievous smile cross her face. She knows I'm scared of heights, but she also knows I won't let her climb a ladder pregnant. I groan, realizing that she has me trapped.

"Fine," I tell her, getting out of the car and slamming the door shut behind me. "I'll help you put the finishing touches on. But don't expect anything else from me today."

She puts the key in the lock and then draws back.

"Close your eyes," she commands.

"Don't be ridiculous." She comes up behind me and places her hand over both of my eyes. "Petal, this is unnecessary."

"I want to see your first impression of the place. It's better if it's a surprise until you get in the door. You need to be at the perfect vantage point to appreciate what it looks like. Keep an open mind and remember – this is different from Rose's shop."

She guides me through the front door and I wait as she positions me just so in what I think is the far corner at the front of the store. Her small hands still cover my eyes. I open them to try to sneak a peek at where we're going and brace myself for what it looks like in here, but I can't see anything through her fingers. Suddenly, she drops them and I see the work she's done.

I'm speechless.

Most of the walls are a soft lilac that practically glows in the light streaming in through the glass at the front of the store. The remaining wall far to the right is a deep navy blue, so dark it looks like charcoal at first glance. Along the bottom third of the wall, she's painted a mural of flowers. It looks like the watercolor flowers she paints on greeting cards but far more vibrant for being done with acrylics. The wooden tables are set up in the back left and back right corners with a row of comfortable chairs lined up just inside the door for waiting clients. I wonder where she got them and how she paid for them before I remember Petal excels at finding secondhand furniture for cheap.

In a pile in the center of the room is a ring covered with gauzy curtains like a mosquito net. This must be what she needs the ladder for.

"What do you think?" she asks, anxiety coloring her voice. "We still need the chairs from Rose, but I think you can get a good idea of what I'm going for here. I also want to get a few lamps with shades to make the lighting a little softer than these overhead lights. I just haven't had time to go to the store. The mural took longer than I thought it would."

"Petal," I say. I don't know what to say about how perfectly she embodied everything I could have needed in this storefront. I walk toward the mural to inspect it. "It is beyond anything I could have imagined."

"Do you mean it?" I turn around to see her face lit up from within. She truly does look like she's glowing, but I think it's more from the compliment and less from the pregnancy. Do pregnant women glow this early on? And exactly *how* pregnant is she after all?

I don't ask any of those questions right now so we can focus on this moment, her achievement in making this place less creepy and more hospitable to actual customers. I look around and notice that the mannequins are gone.

"I sold them," she says as if reading my mind. "A seamstress wanted them for her models."

"Did you decorate the back offices too?" I'm already wandering into the rooms at the back of the store. I notice she has painted the doors and trim the same navy blue as the accent wall. It isn't a choice I would have thought to make, but she has an eye for choosing colors and making a space pop. I have to hand it to her: this place looks far better than I imagined possible when she first brought me here.

"I painted them, but that's about it," she says.

I duck my head into the room and breathe in the scent of new paint. Both offices are a bright shade of cream that makes them feel bigger than the closet-sized offices they are. In the office on the left stands a huge sandwich board sign with delicate paintings that mirror the ones on the wall in the main area. It reads "Answering Life's Questions at The Glass Orb for $30."

"Did you paint this?" I ask, kneeling to look at it closer. Petal trails in behind me and nods. "The Glass Orb?"

"I thought it might be nice to put out on the road so people know you're here when they drive by. I picked this storefront because it's pretty visible from the main road, but you need to let people know you're here. The Mexican restaurant has a sign about margaritas out there and they seem to do fairly well. I thought you could use some representation too. The Glass Orb, like the crystal ball you were reading when you started this work. Do you like it?"

"Everything about this place is absolutely perfect, Petal," I tell her, standing up from my spot on the floor of the office. I note that my knees are still clean when I stand up. We must have done a great job cleaning last week.

"That's good because I've been marketing it," she says, pulling out her phone. "Friday is your first day in business."

"What exactly do you mean by marketing?"

"I made you a social media page and I took out some ads in the *Post and Courier*. I thought about paying for Facebook ads because they get more visibility than your organic reach, but I want to hold onto the budget in case we need it later."

"And what kind of response have you gotten?" Hope swells in me that maybe we can make this work. Petal has more business sense than I gave her credit for when she sprung this shop on me. I hadn't put much thought into marketing yet. In some ways, the store still felt like an abstract thing but seeing it completed makes me feel differently.

"You're up to five hundred likes on Facebook." She beams.

"Let me see," I say, grabbing her phone from her hands. There's no way we could be up to five hundred likes. It took us a year to build up to that number with Rose's shop, and we put some serious effort into marketing. But Petal is right: five hundred people have seen us on Facebook and want updates about our business. Petal used it to reveal bits of her progress in redecorating the store along with advertisements for the services we will offer when we open: tarot card readings, palm readings, chakra alignment, and crystal ball gazing.

"Crystal ball gazing?" I look up at her with my eyebrows raised.

"It's how you got this job in the first place. You're good at reading people. Everything is on the table, remember? You can make a killing off crystal ball gazing. All you have to do is see some murky shapes and guess at what they might be."

"Ah, so I've encountered an area where you might be a skeptic after all."

"Say what you want, but the tarot cards are the real deal. I seem to recall that *your* fortune is coming true after the reading I gave you last week. Do you want me to pull more cards for you so that you can see what's going to come next?"

"I can probably hazard a few guesses at what you'll see." I tap my finger on my chin. "How about true love rekindled and the birth of a new identity?"

"Too on the nose." She smiles. "The tarot cards are *never* that precise. It's all in the interpretation."

"And let me guess. You have the right interpretation that will unlock the keys to my future."

"Naturally."

"I think I'll pass on the reading. Did you want help hanging these curtains or not?"

Petal walks over to the curtains and starts explaining to me her vision for how they will drape across the room if we hang them from the center, creating swags that cascade down from the ceiling. I'm having a hard time picturing it, but after seeing what she's done with the rest of the shop, she likely has a vision I'm too blind to see.

We spend an hour arguing as I climb the ladder slowly and screw the netting to the top of the ceiling. After I finished, we moved the ladder around the room, creating swags with the translucent fabric. The result is something like a circus big top but more elegant. It softens the harsh glare of the overhead lights. The cream color of the fabric perfectly complements the lilac walls and the gauzy feel of it reminds me of the tablecloths Rose favors in her shop. This is a much different aesthetic, but Petal has managed to capture the essence of who I am and what I would want in a storefront. The night is coming on quickly, so we finish up the last touches and walk to the front door.

"Petal," I tell her, looking back at our handiwork. "Thank you. This is really and truly the perfect space for me."

"It's for *us*," she corrects me. "We're in this together from here on out. I know I sprang a lot on you today and it wasn't exactly how I envisioned telling you, but I'm so glad you're doing this with me."

"You didn't exactly give me another choice," I grumble.

She puts her arm around my shoulders and rests her head on my collarbone. Despite every little thing she's done to annoy me recently, I have to admit that I love my sister and that sometimes, she does know exactly what she's doing.

Chapter 13

The last few days of working for Rose seem to fly by. It strikes me as too soon to put the out-of-business sign on the door when Wednesday rolls around, but Rose hangs it in the window without ceremony or fanfare. She leaves the address to my new shop at the bottom of the sign, hopeful that we can attract some of our usual clients to a new location. Rose isn't bitter about the fact that her shop is closing so mine can begin. This is touching and generous. She puts her decorative items in boxes and we haul them out to her car. By the time we leave on Wednesday afternoon, the store is just as empty as it was when Rose first came to this location three years ago.

We invite Petal over to have lunch on the cold tile floor – this achievement of a successful shop belongs just as much to Petal as it does to us. She was my guinea pig when I was learning to do this, and she often brought her friends along to have their fortunes read (gratis, at first and as paying clients later).

"Are you sure you want to do this?" I ask Rose. But even as I ask the question, I realize we are too far gone for her to change her mind. The shop is empty, the lease has run out, and the time has come for all of us to move on to the next thing.

"I've seen the future," Rose says, an air of mystery in her voice. There's a small quiver in her words, betraying her feelings about the end of this era in her life. This shop was her baby, and she sacrificed for it over the years at great personal cost. She invested her money and, maybe more importantly, her time. "It's time for me to pass the baton."

103

"I wouldn't be able to do this without you. You took a chance on me all those years ago."

"You were destined for this," she says, her voice more certain than I have heard it all day. She looks around at the empty room. The only things left are the velvet chairs that Petal has come to claim for our new store. We bought Rose lunch from Philly's as payment for the furniture; it was the only thing she would accept.

"I wish I shared your certainty," I mumble.

"We already have people coming by the store," Petal announces. "I had two women come by while I was putting the finishing touches on things today. This is going to be just fine, Essie. If you want, we can read your cards to prove it."

"I don't see what reading my cards is going to prove. You know those aren't real."

"All I know is that last time I read your cards, they slowly came true. New opportunities, new life. All you need is a new relationship and I can feel it on the horizon for you. Maybe it isn't Mark, but he isn't the only man in town. You might as well let us read your cards for you now to put these doubts to rest."

"She's right, Esmerelda," Rose volunteers. I roll my eyes at her, angry that the two of them are ganging up on me when they know how I feel about fortunetelling.

"Fine." I force a smile on my face to show that I'm game. I pull the tarot deck Petal made me out of my bag. "Read my cards, Petal."

"Shuffle them," she commands.

I mix the cards up haphazardly. Petal closes her eyes and feels the tarot deck in her hands when I hand it back to her. I know she's picturing the transfer of my energy to the cards, the solemn rite of letting her intuition guide her to make an accurate reading – or as accurate as something fake can be, anyway.

"What should we know about the future?" she muses, as she cuts the deck and pulls the top card. "Ace of Pentacles."

"Interesting choice," I tell her. I know Petal wants the full experience of doing a reading, so I ask, "But what does it mean?"

"The Ace of Pentacles card represents a new endeavor where finances will increase and you'll find success faster than you thought possible."

"Well, that settles it," Rose announces. "Your store is going to be a smashing success."

"Maybe we should go put it together and get everything set up for opening day. Friday is only a day and a half away," Petal says.

"I'll tell you what," I say. "I'll take the chairs over to the shop and put the final touches on things. You have really gone above and beyond, Petal. Why don't you take the rest of the afternoon off and hang out with Rose?"

Petal's face brightens at the possibility of spending a little time with Rose. I wonder how their relationship will fare when the roles are reversed and Petal is the one in charge of running the day-to-day aspects of the store. She tosses me the keys to the truck she rented. Rose and I carry the chairs out to the bed of the truck while Petal supervises.

Now that the secret is out of the bag, I start to notice all of the things Petal *hasn't* been doing. She didn't paint the storefront, but Turner did. She didn't climb the ladder to hang the curtains, but I did. She cleaned, but not with the most toxic chemicals. She didn't get down on her hands and knees to scrub the floor. All this time, she's been protecting the little life inside of her without ever letting on to the fact that she is harboring new life. It strikes me as significant that this is the first secret Petal has ever successfully kept from me. I wonder how much longer she had intended to keep it from me if the apartment search hadn't blown up.

I give her a hug goodbye at the store and climb in the truck to head over to the new store with the velvet chairs getting windblown in the bed of the truck. I navigate carefully around the corners to avoid upsetting the chairs in the truck bed. I don't want them to accidentally topple out of the truck and into the street. Petal and I can't afford new furniture for the shop, not with a new apartment lease pending. We still haven't decided whether we'll live together or not.

My phone rings and I pick it up, expecting Petal to give me some last-minute instruction on how to set up the space in her absence.

"Esmerelda." I pull the phone away from my ear and look at the caller ID. Mark.

"Did we not have the same conversation a few days ago about how I might 'get the wrong idea?'" I try to make my use of air quotes obvious over the phone.

"Esmerelda, I didn't mean that we should stop seeing each other. I just meant that we never had any discussions about being exclusive."

"And let me get this straight: you want to see other people, but you would also like to see me on occasion when your other plans fall through."

"You're twisting my words."

"Mark, I really do like you but I'm not interested in playing games. Maybe I wasn't totally clear on that when I set up my online dating profile. At the moment, I have bigger fish to fry with my sister. The truth is I just don't have time for someone who has no time for me."

"If that's how you feel," he says. "Let me know if you change your mind."

The phone clicks as he hangs up. I feel empowered, which is saying a lot because my sister is ruining my independence at every turn.

I grab my turquoise key and unlock the front doors, propping them open with the ancient phonebook we have been using as a doorstop. I carry all four of the chairs into the space, arranging them in various patterns to see what works best with Petal's layout. She has divided the open floor plan into several small sections. The chairs are meant to be for the fortuneteller and the clients who are receiving a reading; we bought less luxurious chairs for the waiting clients.

"Knock, knock." A voice comes from behind me and causes me to jump. "I hope I'm not interrupting anything."

Turner is standing in the doorway to the store, one hand poised as if to knock on the glass of the front door. I want to have less of a reaction to him, but I can't help the way my heart speeds up when I look at those strong biceps beneath a short-sleeve button-down. I chastise myself for even thinking of him that way. My face flushes as if I've been caught with my hand in the cookie jar.

"Petal told me you'd be here," he says.

"It seems like one of us has to be here around the clock," I tell him. "Come in and sit down for a minute. I'm just rearranging furniture. You can tell me what you think."

His head swivels as he takes in the entire room. I forgot that he hadn't seen it since he came to help Petal roll out paint on the walls. The transformation with the mural, the curtains, and even the new-to-us furniture must make this seem like an entirely new space.

"It looks great in here, Ess," he says.

"Petal should take the credit for it. The only thing I've done is arrange the chairs," I laugh. "But I could use a break from all this work. What brings you by?"

"You used to want to go back to school, to support you and Petal both on one salary. Does this gig really pay well enough for you to do that?"

"It apparently pays well enough that Petal had enough money to pay for this lease in full with the checks I've been sending her. If you had asked me before, I might have said no but I have a new appreciation for it."

"Will you read my fortune?" he asks.

"I don't really believe in this," I explain.

"I don't think you should really tell people that when you're trying to run a business. Let me be your first customer. After all, I'm the reason Petal found this place."

I laugh at his obvious attempt to persuade me to read his cards, but give in to him anyway. The tarot cards are still in my bag from earlier, so I pull them out and sit down on the opposite side of the table from him.

"Shuffle them," I instruct him. He mixes the deck up with expert hands, not even bending the cards in the process. Turner hands the deck back to me and it's like I can feel the electricity of the cards in my hand, all of the places where his skin brushed against them. "We'll pull three cards in a standard reading: one for the past, present, and future."

With that explanation, I peel the first three cards off the top of the deck and arrange them face down in front of him.

"Your past is the Three of Swords. This symbolizes that you have had something serious in your past. Maybe it was a romantic relationship or a friendship, but it has since been fractured. There is a possibility of mending fences, but it will come at great personal cost to you." I try not to swallow hard at how on the nose this reading is.

He nods and I flip over the next card.

"Your present is the Wheel of Fortune. This card symbolizes that you are in a time of great transformation. One phase of your life is ending, but a new one is just about to open up. It suggests that something major is happening right now, but the area of your life where the change occurs is unknown.

"Your future –"

"Don't tell me the future," he says. "I've changed my mind. I think I'm okay with just knowing the past and the present. This is scarily accurate and I'd hate to spoil it for myself.

"The truth is that anyone can read the cards because it's so subjective. I find that a lot of people come in to have their cards read and then shape their future to make it align with the reading they got. In other words, it's a self-fulfilling prophecy. Maybe it's for the best that we leave your future unknown."

I shuffle the cards back into the deck and put it in my bag.

"But I don't think you came here for a reading," I say, turning my attention back to him.

"No, I suppose I didn't." He looks thoughtful for a moment. "I think I just came to check up on you. Petal dropped a huge bomb on you and I wanted to know how you were holding up."

I sigh and run a hand over my face, buying time before I have to answer him. The truth is I still don't know what I'm going to do about her announcement. In the past, I've always taken care of Petal but I never banked on having to take care of a baby too.

"I'm really not sure," I finally announce, disappointed in how honest I'm being with him. I wish I could pretend everything was fine, just fine. But I know that if I put on airs that Petal and I seem to have worked all of this out, he'll be able to fish out the lie in an instant. It would ruin whatever tentative strands of trust are starting to weave between us.

That makes me stop to question my intention with him. *Are* we starting to get close again after so many years apart? The truth is that I know absolutely nothing about his personal life other than what he does for a living these days. There have been things that grew us, shaped us, and changed us as we were apart. The problem is all those extra entrapments seem to come away when he's standing here in front of me. I think of his hand on my lower back at the restaurant and wish he would touch me again, a small comfort in the midst of Petal's hurricane. I shake my head to dispel the thought and he looks at me quizzically.

"You always took care of Petal." He looks almost sympathetic, his gaze softening. "It must be hard for you to reconcile the fact that you can't take care of this for her."

"I don't *want* to take care of this for her," I finally say, realizing the truth of it as I speak it. "I want to take care of Petal, yes. But only because there's no one else in the world looking out for her. She had Jason, and then that seems to have imploded. What am I supposed to do with a baby? And now we have this store to worry about too."

I can sense myself gaining momentum with the list of ways Petal has taken my life off its trajectory. I swallow hard to keep the words from spewing out over the neatly defined lines of our friendly relationship. We *used* to be lovers, I remind myself. He doesn't need to hear every detail of how my relationship with Petal is going off the rails.

"At a certain point, you're going to have to let Petal make her own life decisions."

Our conversation resonates with truth, and I let it fall heavy over me. As far as I know, the only reason Turner and I aren't together right now is because I prioritized Petal over him three years ago. I love my sister and would gladly do it all over again, but I'm also acutely aware of what I sacrificed to keep her happy, to care for her. My life could be different right now: a beautiful house, a dog, maybe a child of my own. Instead, I'm telling people fortunes and scamming them out of their money while thinking about how I'm going to provide for myself, Petal, and now a new baby.

"I think you're right," I finally tell him. "But I also know I can't just push her to figure it out. I'm thinking about moving in with her, to help out with the baby."

I see the flicker of something like recognition dawn on his face before his expression turns hard. All of the warmth and empathy I felt radiating off of him when he came in here is completely gone. He pulls his phone out and makes a show of checking the time.

"I should be going. I have another client to meet up with this afternoon. That place I showed you guys yesterday is still on the market, but it won't last long."

"What did I do?" I don't give myself time to think through the conversation this will bring about, acting entirely off impulse. The moment I say it aloud, I realize that I might not want the answer. I shouldn't be getting close to Turner when my entire life is being upended by my sister, but I can't help myself. He is the closest thing

I have to a relationship, my only link to who I used to be apart from Petal.

"Nothing ever changes, Esmerelda," he says. He uses my full name rather than his nickname.

"What is that supposed to mean?"

"Nothing." He shakes his head. "Everything. I don't know."

I wait for a minute while he processes what he wants to say. Sometimes, it takes Turner a minute to collect his thoughts. He squeezes his eyes shut and pinches the bridge of his nose while he thinks, a tic he picked up from his father.

"I thought it might have been a sign when Petal reached out to me, that she was out living her own life for a change and was trying to make up all those years you sacrificed for her. I think in her own way, she was. But you can't help yourself from swooping in to save her when things stop going according to the plan."

"I don't know what I'm supposed to do here," I argue, feeling the rage boil up in me. "Petal literally has no one to rely on *except* for me now, and she's about to have a baby."

"I know." His voice rises a few decibels, but then he takes a deep breath. In a lower voice, he says, "I just thought maybe this could be different."

There is a sudden hollowness in my stomach, the place where butterflies used to live. Now, the only thing that remains is a barren wasteland. The truth is I let myself want Turner in a way that I had been conscious to keep at bay with Mark. I wanted him to rest his hand on my lower back, to walk me to my car, to help me provide for my sister. We fell effortlessly back into rhythm after all of these years apart, but there is no erasing the past between us.

"I should go," he finally says when I don't answer him.

I watch him turn and leave the store without a backward glance.

Chapter 14

"Today is the day," Petal sings as she puts her key in the lock and sweeps into the store at 10:00 AM. I'm still nursing my second cup of coffee, but I feel almost as exuberant as Petal does. All along, I've been the skeptic who wasn't sure whether this store was a good idea or another one of Petal's doomed entrepreneurial endeavors. The truth is that Petal has sunk so much money into this place that I'm now vicariously living through her ambition to make this successful.

We lock the door behind us as we go around turning on lights and putting our things away. There is a full half-hour before the doors officially open, but we came in early to ensure that every detail is taken care of before the first guest arrives. I fuss with the tablecloths, the placement of the chairs, the mood lighting in the corner of the room designed for palm reading. By the time I look up fifteen minutes before the store is set to open, I see three customers milling about outside the front door.

"Ready to roll?" Petal asks with a grin.

I nod and take a seat at one of the tables in the corner. We've already worked out that Petal will be like the hostess at a restaurant. She will get people in line for services, position them in the waiting area, and let me know who is here and whose turn it is for a reading. As she starts to talk with the first woman in line, I wonder how Petal learned to do all of this. She has had only a couple of weeks to drum up business and yet, she's doing better than I ever thought possible. This is a real-world skill she seems to have mastered.

The morning is spent reading tarot cards for the three people who showed up as soon as the doors opened, followed by another two people just before lunch. We have steady traffic all day until the lunch hour hits when a lull pops in. Petal takes the respite in customers as a chance to count the money in the drawer. I don't know how to tell her that there is less than $200 in there because all we've done is five readings. It will take more than this boom of traffic to make the kind of money she needs to keep the wheels on this place.

"Do you think we'll be able to sustain more traffic?" she frets. "You've been busy all day, but you're only one person. Maybe we should call Rose in so we can read twice as many people."

"There aren't twice as many people *waiting* for a reading, Petal." I soften my voice. I don't want to upset her when she's clearly put a lot of effort into growing this business. "It's just the first day. It takes time to build up clientele."

"I just want it to be *perfect* today. I have a little surprise for you."

"I don't know if I can take any more surprises, especially from you."

"This one is more for *us*," she corrects. "I might have finagled a review from the *Post and Courier* for opening day."

"Seriously?"

"They didn't promise who they would send, so I don't know what to look for. I want the place to look busy because that shows we're doing well. On the flip side, I don't want them to have to wait *too* long for their reading because it could be bad for the review."

"I think it will be just fine," I reassure her.

Internally, I'm panicking a little bit. A prominent review from the *Post and Courier* carries tremendous weight with the local crowd. What if I give them a reading that doesn't sound so positive? What if I don't tell them the exact fortune they want to hear or give them an interpretation loose enough to view their present circumstances? I take a deep breath and remind myself that I've been doing this for a long time. I have enough intuition to read the room and adjust a reading if I need to. However, I still think that the least Petal could have done was warn me that we had a reviewer coming today.

We stare out at the parking lot together, waiting for the next person to arrive but not wanting to look too eager when the white minivan pulls up in front of the store.

"Maybe this is her," Petal says. "Go ahead and take your seat. I'll bring her to you."

"Maybe you shouldn't be on your feet so much," I tell her, gesturing toward her swelling stomach but she laughs and waves me off. I go sit down in the corner behind the sheer curtain, but I can tell this woman isn't here for a reading. She's carrying a huge vase of sunflowers, wrapped in a burlap ribbon.

"I'm looking for an Esmerelda," she says. I stand up from the corner of the room and walk to the front table. She acknowledges me with a little chuckle. I almost know what she's about to say before she says it. "That's one heck of a name for a psychic."

I smile politely at her as she finishes her laughter and hands me the vase of flowers. I thank her and she leaves me with the glass vase. Petal is next to me in an instant, demanding to know who I should thank for this gorgeous arrangement. The small white envelope has been sealed with navy blue wax, and I pop it open to see for myself who could have sent these. I know it wasn't Mark, but I'm not sure who else would have the thought. Maybe Rose sent them, I think. She is one of those people who always does thoughtful things like sending flowers. The card reads: *I still believe in you. – Turner*

"What is *that* supposed to mean?" Petal asks, her eyes narrowed. She is like a bloodhound, sniffing out any clues of romance that have been going on underneath her nose.

"We had a little... disagreement when I brought the chairs over Wednesday. It seems that things aren't as different as we had maybe thought they were."

"Were you guys going to get back together?" Petal is staring at me, eyes open wide. It's like she hadn't yet considered this possibility when she invited him back into our lives with this store first, and now her new apartment. Like it wasn't her master plan all along. "I thought..."

"I didn't think we were going to get back together. And we certainly aren't now. Nothing much has changed over the past few years. We're still the same people we always were."

Petal hums under her breath but doesn't say anything. I'm waiting for her to think through what she wants to say. I can tell something is hovering just on the tip of her tongue.

"I thought maybe if you two saw each other again, he would break things off with his girlfriend and maybe you could finally be together."

The blood pounds in my ears and the knot in my stomach intensifies at Petal's revelation. At no point during the conversations between Turner and me did he ever let on that he might be seeing someone. This should have been information he shared when we got dinner together or when he popped by the store to help paint, or even yesterday when he told me that things would never be different.

No, I don't suppose they will be different now.

"He never mentioned a girlfriend," I finally say, realizing Petal expects a response.

She nods as if it makes sense that he would withhold this detail from me.

"I think they're pretty serious," she says. "He was talking about buying a house."

"He's a real estate agent, Petal," I scoff. "He probably *does* want to buy a house, but that doesn't necessarily mean he's serious with the woman he's seeing. Besides, he has the right to see whoever he wants. We weren't going to get back together just because you have a sudden penchant for real estate."

"I don't know," she muses. "He did send you a bouquet of your favorite flowers."

Petal plucks them from my hand and walks over to the table where I do my readings. She sets them up on the black tablecloth and I have to admit they look nice there. I tell myself a little bit of greenery is all the place needed to feel more alive. I try not to think about the conflicting feelings inside of me: joy that Turner thinks about me enough to send flowers on our opening day and despair that it can't mean anything more than just flowers.

Petal finishes arranging the flowers on the table when a young woman walks in and asks for a palm reading. Petal nudges her toward me and I take her hand in mind, warm skin on warm skin. I close my eyes and try to push the thought of a reviewer far from my mind. This is not the time to think about publicity or failed relationships. This is the time to focus completely on the person in front of me who wants me to tell them something about their life that they don't yet know – or something they *do* know and haven't yet admitted to.

The rest of the afternoon flies by in a blur. We have a steady stream of customers come in once the lunch hour is over and we finish the day with almost $700 in the cash register. Petal locks the door before she counts it up, but she can't resist holding it all in her hands and bringing it up to her nose to breathe in the scent of financial freedom. I hope nobody can see in through the glass because this would be an opportune time for us to get robbed.

"Let's get ready to go home, Petal," I tell her, tossing her the cash bag so we can make a deposit at the bank on the way home. "I hate having this much cash in here. We should switch to card only."

"But then we'd have to pay the transaction fees," she argues. "I've thought of everything."

And for the first time in my life, I have to say I'm genuinely surprised at just how much of this Petal really *has* thought about. Maybe she isn't as helpless as I've always thought her to be.

Chapter 15

I'm running behind the next morning. I was up too late thinking about how the first day went, anxious about what might await us on the second day. Fortunately, we have Rose coming in as reinforcements if the day proves to be as busy as opening day. I spent my night wondering how we could keep up a steady stream of business and bring in enough money for both of us, plus Petal. Petal had done such a great job advertising our place, but I wondered how long she would be able to keep the steady stream of clients coming. I'm just slipping my loose-fitting black t-shirt over my head when Petal knocks aggressively on the door.

"You *have* to see this," she yells from the hall.

"I'll be out in a minute," I tell her. She thumps back toward the kitchen and starts to open and shut cabinet doors, slamming things around as she goes. It doesn't sound like our morning is off to a great start, and I dread the idea of spending the entire day with her in the shop. At least we have Rose to balance things out.

I turn off the light and go to face Petal's wrath. Petal throws the newspaper at me and stares while I scan what made her so upset: the review of our store went live. Even from the headline, I can tell this isn't going to be good news for business:

New Psychic Shop Scams People Out of Hard-Earned Money

So-called psychic Esmerelda has opened the doors to a new business here in the Lowcountry, but it might not be as good for the economy as it sounds. She promises that you can learn your future and fortune with a few tarot cards or maybe a palm reading. I visited her shop to see if it was true – and now you don't have to. The jig is up: Esmerelda and her shop, The Glass Orb, are completely fraudulent.

The article goes on for another few paragraphs, but I don't have the heart to read them. It's obvious from this introduction that nothing this Ryan character says is going to be positive. I try to place the person who wrote this review with the steady stream of customers we had yesterday. There was an equal split of men and women who came by. Petal didn't get their names upon arrival, and I didn't remember a Ryan in the crowd. It was obvious he didn't like the fortune I read, but I can't recall reading anything negative yesterday.

"This is going to be so bad for business," Petal moans when I set the paper down on the kitchen island between us.

I pour myself a cup of coffee and try to rack my brain for what I could say to make this seem a little better. Unfortunately, the words simply aren't coming to me. Petal is right: this review isn't what we needed to get more people through the door. Everyone in this town reads the *Post and Courier*; it won't take long for the word to get out that our shop is a sham. Even though I knew it was a sham from the beginning, I didn't want *other* people to think so.

"Maybe no one will read it," I offer after a sip of coffee.

Petal shakes her head and tosses the newspaper in the trash. "We were supposed to get a positive review. Now what are we going to do?"

This was something I had been training for my entire life. Petal needs a little redirection to think about this in a more positive light. It doesn't matter that I think the review is bad news for The Glass Orb just as much as she does. I have to put on a positive face and give her something to work with.

"We're going to go to work and do the same thing we did yesterday," I tell her, placing one hand on each of her shoulders and forcing her to look at me. "This is *one* person's opinion. It doesn't matter. We're going to keep showing up and we'll find another way to drum up business. This newspaper is not the only thing in town."

Petal closes her eyes, takes a deep breath, and nods. When she opens them again, she no longer looks like she's on the verge of collapsing under the weight of this negative review.

"We need to get a new reviewer out," she says, wandering away to find her laptop.

"What we need right now is to leave for work," I correct her. "You can work on that from the store. Rose is with me today so you can hang out in the back office."

Petal and I rush to grab last-minute items that we forgot to bring yesterday: phone chargers, paperbacks for the lulls, snacks. I stuff a tote bag with all of our must-haves and we walk out the door to get to the shop. When we pull up, no people are waiting for us outside the door like there were yesterday.

"Don't you see?" Petal exclaims as she unlocks the door. "That review has already jinxed us."

"Leave the door unlocked for Rose," I tell her, spotting Rose's car navigating into the lot. "I'll lock it behind her until we're ready to open for the day."

"You might as well just leave it unlocked," Petal sniffs. "It's not like we're going to have any customers today."

Rose walks through the door, her perfume announcing her immediately. She always smells like freshly cut flowers and incense because she burns it almost around the clock in her house. The thing is that Rose does believe in tapping into her intuition in ways that I don't. She uses all of the tools she can to dig deep into her intuition: incense, crystals, essential oils, you name it. I wonder if her dedication to the craft is why her shop flourished while ours might just be dead on the vine after this review. Maybe it would have been different if *Rose* had read the fortunes instead of me.

"Ladies," Rose announces herself, switching the lock over the front door behind her. "I've had a vision this morning."

I roll my eyes, knowing this has something to do with her morning tarot cards. Rose pulls her cards every morning as a way to see what the day will bring and what type of energy she needs to bring to the table. No matter what she saw, Petal is likely to read into it given the review.

"Petal, you seem to be facing a dilemma of some kind," she continues. "You will get to the bottom of it this morning and things will turn around for you."

"How did you know?" Petal's eyes glisten like she's on the verge of tears.

"The cards never lie." she says. Rose probably just looked at her closely. She believes in using everything around her when she makes a reading: the clothes a person is wearing, their energy, the items they choose to set on the table. Even the cards themselves act as a sort of talisman that tells her precisely what she needs to hear.

Petal nods at her as if this makes perfect sense. Maybe to someone a little less skeptical, it does make sense. She rolls her shoulders back and straightens her spine, putting off an air of newly inspired confidence.

"I have some phone calls to make. You two keep things running," she announces, going into the office on the left and closing the door behind her.

"What's the deal with her?" Rose whispers when the door is shut. I unlock the front door for the customers who aren't lining up outside and slide into one of the chairs designed for waiting clients.

"She arranged for a review at the *Post and Courier*," I tell her.

"I remember. She was so excited about it, but she wanted to keep it a secret from you."

"Well, that review came back in this morning."

"Bad news?"

"*Very* bad news," I say. "It told everyone that the shop is a fraud – maybe more to the point, that *I'm* a fraud."

"It's the energy you put out into the universe," Rose says sympathetically. "I've warned you about this before. When you don't take the cards seriously, you set people up to tell you that there is no science behind this, no art to it."

"You know, I don't need a lecture on this right now."

"I'm sorry," she says, coming to sit in the chair beside me. "What can I do to help remedy it?"

"Can you take over the readings for this morning?"

"Of course," she says, getting up and walking to the table where the magic happens. She notices the flowers on the table and plucks the card out of the basket. "These are beautiful. Turner sent you these?"

I nod.

"I think there's something more there," she says. "Why don't we read *your* cards and see what it is?"

"It's nothing," I tell her. "It can *never* be anything. That's in the past. In the meantime, we're stuck in this terrible pattern while we search for an apartment for Petal."

"I don't know," she says. "I can feel the energy of this card and it doesn't feel like nothing."

"Do you want to read my cards?" I ask her, desperate enough to change the subject that I'm willing to go along with anything. I pull up the chair reserved for clients and sit down, shuffling the deck she hands across to me.

"Clear it with the crystal," she prompts me.

I tap the deck twice with the small rose quartz crystal Rose always keeps in her pocket. She even charges them with the moon when the cycle is right. She takes the deck from my hand and closes her eyes to feel the vibration and energy of the cards. Part of me wishes she had used my deck, the one Petal made for me. There's something special about a deck that was not only given to you but *made* for you.

"What does your love life hold?" Rose asks the deck, cuts it once, and pulls a card from the top of the pile. "Ace of Cups. A good sign for budding romance."

"You know as well as I do that that card is not necessarily a good thing."

"But it could be perfect for your current love life."

I think about Rose's interpretation of the card placed face up on the table in front of me. I sigh and pick the card up to examine its artistic interpretation of the deck. A huge part of me wishes Rose's interpretation of the card was accurate: that there was some kind of future between Turner and me. But then I remind myself that he's in a serious relationship, one that he failed to mention when we had dinner together; when he was helping get The Glass Orb in order; and even when we had our fight about how I always take care of Petal. There is no future here for us – the same as I determined the last time we ended our relationship.

The front door chimes and someone walks in, prompting me to rise from the table and try to forget about the reading Rose just gave me. As much as I know this shop is a sham, I still want to believe that something positive could come from my life.

"Welcome," I tell the young woman, realizing that she looks sort of familiar. "How can I help you?"

"I'd like my money back." She waves a copy of the *Post and Courier* around haphazardly.

"I'm sorry, but we don't do refunds." We never really talked about this, but we can't issue a refund to everyone whose reading doesn't come true. Knowing we have no real power to tell the future, it doesn't make sense to give people their money back when a fake tarot card reading gives them bad advice.

Petal must have overheard the conversation because she emerges from the back office with a stricken expression on her face. She takes in the angry young woman with her sleek brunette hair pinned back in a clip, the newspaper fluttering around her face.

"You want a refund for your reading yesterday?" Petal asks, her eyes wide. It's clear she hadn't yet considered the full implications of this review.

"It says right *here* that this place is fraudulent. Their words, not mine," she says, pointing emphatically to the review in the newspaper. "I can't believe I wasted my money on this scam."

"Of course," Petal says, walking to the cash register. From the wooden way she walks to the drawer and the monotone sound of her voice, I can tell she isn't sure what else to do. I have to admit that this girl would be extremely bad for business if anyone else came in while she was here demanding her money back. Maybe Petal has the right idea, but how many more people will ask for their money back if we cave right now?

The girl takes her money with a huff and storms out of the store. I watch her walk back to her car where she gets inside, slams the door shut, and sits to count the five-dollar bills Petal gave her. Honestly, I'm surprised she didn't count it in front of us to make sure we weren't ripping her off after the way she waved that newspaper around reminding us that we were fraudulent.

"I have a solution to the problem," Petal says after the girl drives away. She walks to the front door and looks out into the empty parking lot. "This review is going to be worse for business than I anticipated, but I got them to say they'll send a reporter out for a second chance."

"Petal, that isn't going to change anything. This place *is* fraudulent," I remind her.

"Just because you don't believe in the energy of the universe doesn't make this place any less real to our customers," Petal corrects me. She has a point. The people we serve *do* believe in the magic of what we do here. Maybe that deserves more weight than I have ever given credit. I nod so that she'll continue.

"They are going to come back out, and I need you two to be at the top of your game. This Ryan guy is going to come in here and I need him to have the best fortune he's ever had. Windfalls of cash, a thriving love life, you name it. I know the cards are subjective, and I need you to be the ones to guide the reading toward success," she explains.

"You're asking us to lie to every guy who comes in here on the off chance it might be the guy from the *Post and Courier*?" I ask. I can hardly believe it. Petal believes in the sanctity of the cards, so it seems strange that she would tell us to skew the readings.

"Just until the review comes out," she says. "I'm going to go try to do some damage control in the office. Will you two be okay up here by yourselves today? With this review, I'm guessing we aren't likely to be terribly busy."

Petal retreats to the office, leaving Rose and me sitting in the foyer of the store. I'm struck by the realization that this feels different than it did when we were at Rose's shop. When I was reading cards and telling fortunes for her, I never had to worry about the business side. If we got a bad review, I didn't have to do damage control. I didn't handle the marketing or the social media. I suddenly feel the huge and heavy weight of responsibility on my shoulders.

Rose must sense what I'm thinking, because she says, "It's a lot to think about, isn't it?"

I sit down in the client chair facing the door, but the parking lot remains empty. In fact, the parking lot remains empty for most of the day. We see two men: one older with a graying beard and a beer belly who wanted to know if he would get a sudden windfall of cash; one on the younger side with a clean-cut look and a baby face who wanted to know about his love life. Rose read them both spectacular fortunes. We also had three women come by, but we treated them the same as we did every other client: we read in the cards only what the cards would tell us.

At the end of the day, we locked up the front doors and bid goodbye to Rose. Petal and I stayed in the storefront in the dim lighting, hoping that nobody could see through the windows in the dark. She grabbed the drawer out of the cash register and took it to the back office to count it. When she emerged, I could tell she realized what a mistake this entire ordeal was. The Glass Orb wasn't going to be turning a profit any time soon.

"We made less than two hundred dollars today," she says. I nod, tallying up the five readings we did while Petal was holed up back here in the office. "How am I going to pay Rose for her work today on just two hundred dollars?"

"Just give her what we owe her," I tell her gently. "You and I will have to take the pay cut."

"I have a *baby* on the way," Petal reminds me. "We aren't going to be able to take the pay cut every single day."

"Are you ready to talk about the baby?" I ask her, realizing that this is the first time she's brought it up since she sprung the news on me in the apartment last week. I didn't want to pressure her into talking about it more than she wanted to. I had the sense that she was still trying to figure things out and that she would talk about it when she was ready.

Petal huffs and sits down in the leather executive chair behind the desk. "Can you turn off the lights in the shop and shut the office door so no one can see in here?"

The mood lighting clicks off with a flick of the switch, and I shut the door to the office to seal us in. I take the seat across the desk from Petal and wait for her to talk to me.

"What do you want to know?' she finally asks.

"How about we start with the basics?" I try to sound neutral, but I'm dying to ask her the questions that have been simmering in my mind for days. "When are you due?"

"March 14."

"That's six months from now," I tell her, incredulous. "How long have you known and you didn't tell me?"

She cringes. Petal goes on to tell me that the pregnancy was an accident: she had missed a couple of birth control pills without realizing it until it was too late. Jason never wanted to have kids; he was content with their lives as they were, enjoying their double-income, no-kid status. When he found out she was pregnant, he wanted her to have an abortion, but Petal refused. That refusal was the reason they were no longer together, the reason she no longer had a place to live, and the reason we were in this predicament at The Glass Orb together now.

"Why would you keep this all from me?" I try not to sound as wounded as I feel. "You always tell me everything."

"Because I knew you would want to fix it," she explains, looking away from me. "A baby. That isn't something I wanted you to fix. You've *already* tried to fix it. Don't you see?"

"How did I try to fix it?"

"You offered to move in with me because you don't think I'm capable of taking care of a baby entirely on my own." She pauses while I let the weight of that sink in. "I'm not saying I don't appreciate your thought, but there are some things I just need to do on my own."

"You're right," I finally say. "I shouldn't try to fix it for you. You're old enough to be your own person now, even if it's hard for me to see that sometimes."

We sit there in companionable silence for a little while. It feels like something momentous has shifted in our relationship. I'm no longer in the role of having to care for Petal, and she is on her own for the first time in her adult life. She bounced from me directly to Jason and hasn't ever truly been on her own – and now she has a baby to cope with too. I wonder how she will fare, but then I remember that she's already accomplished so much.

"Would you like to see what I'm working on?" she asks, changing the subject. She shuffles some papers around on the desk and pulls out a sheet of watercolor paper. "Your story inspired this one."

She hands the paper over to me and I study the painting. A woman sits behind a crystal ball with the colors swirling in the glass in front of her. Even I have to admit, she captured the essence of me extremely well in a medium that doesn't lend itself well to minute details. But the crystal ball is the highlight of the piece.

"We should hang this," I tell her. "It would be the perfect décor for the room."

She blushes and takes the paper away from me, studying it herself. For the first time, I can see how much she's grown as a person, as an adult. I wanted to keep her small and childlike, but I can see now that she's been pushing against that from the very beginning. Maybe it was time to start thinking about myself more and Petal less.

Maybe Turner was right.

Chapter 16

When we get home from the shop, Petal sets up her watercolors on the dining room table where she has the best light. I head straight to the bedroom to get a little space to process everything that's happened today: the bad review, the lack of traffic, lying to clients, and Petal insisting that I don't fix her problems for her. I find myself curled up in bed with my phone in my hand, wanting to call the one person who may understand exactly what it feels like for me to let Petal go. Even Rose would never understand the amount I had sacrificed for Petal to have a decent life.

Turner was the only one who would understand.

And I didn't feel like I *should* call him, not now that I knew he had a steady girlfriend. This thought felt like pressing my thumb down in a purple bruise, painful and tender. What had I thought when we went to dinner? That there was some kind of future for us? That he would have waited around for me to finally come to terms with my sister's independence and come running back to him? I feel stupid for thinking it, but part of me *does* believe that's what was going on when we went to dinner.

I can't help myself. I dial his number.

"I never got around to thanking you for the flowers," I tell him when he answers. "Things have been so busy at the store that it just slipped my mind. But they were beautiful. We put them right on the table so we can see them whenever we do a reading."

I'm rambling, but I don't seem to know how to stop the words from coming. I take a deep breath and pause, waiting for his response.

"I remembered that sunflowers used to be your favorite," he says. "I hope they still are."

A pregnant pause fills the line as he clears his throat. I take a deep breath in and say what I called him to say, even if it doesn't repair the damage to the relationship between us.

"I should—"

"You were right," I cut him off.

"I was right? That might be the first time I've ever heard those words come out of your mouth." His deep laugh echoes in my ears and I feel the sound reverberate through my whole body. "But I'm going to need you to be a little more specific."

"I take care of Petal," I explain. "I do everything for her. It's time I start letting her make some of her own decisions."

Turner sighs into the phone and I wait for a response.

"I wish you had come to that realization two years ago."

"I don't think she was capable of it two years ago, but she is now." I pause and let his words sink in. Could they mean what they sound like they mean? "Maybe you're right. Maybe she always has been capable of it and I just never allowed her to show it."

"Ess," Turner starts. "She's *always* been capable of doing this. But you have this issue of needing to control everything. Maybe it's time for you to let that habit go for good."

I let his words hang there for a moment, unsure what to say in response.

"I should go," he says and I nod before I realize that he can't hear my response.

"Me too," I say.

"Good luck with The Glass Orb. I believe in you," he says and then hangs up.

I throw myself back against the pillows and stare up at the ceiling. In a fit of rage, I take my phone and hurl it against the wall on the opposite side of the room. How much different would my life be right now if I had taken Turner's advice two years ago instead of today? Is it possible that we would still be together? He seems to think we would. But if we were truly meant to be, wouldn't we salvage our relationship now that I decided to let go of my toxic habits?

My phone falls to the floor with a crash and I bury my face in the pillows and scream. Petal knocks on the door and then lets herself in when I don't respond. I didn't realize I was loud enough for her to hear me in the dining room. Part of me forgot she was here at all.

"Essie, what's wrong?" Petal climbs into the bed with me and slips under the covers. Our heads are on the same pillow, facing each other, just like we used to do when we were little and shared a bedroom.

"I thought—" I never make it further because the tears start to come in earnest. This might be the first time Petal has seen me cry since our mother's funeral. She looks alarmed but then her gaze softens and she pulls me into her, nestling my head against her collarbone.

"Is this about the store?"

I shake my head and let out another sob.

"Turner," she surmises, and I nod. "Maybe it's time for you to grieve what could have been. I don't remember you shedding a single tear when you guys broke up."

"He was right all along," I mumble. "What if I could have seen that sooner?"

"What was he right about?"

"I *do* try to take care of you instead of letting you be your own person." I pull back from her, look her full in the face, and brush the tears from the corners of my eyes. "You're an adult, Petal. You should be able to make your own decisions without your sister telling you how to run your life."

"I've been trying to tell you that for a long time," she says, her voice low and sympathetic. "You put too much pressure on yourself to fix things for everyone around you."

"I can't tell you what to do with this baby. Maybe it's time for you to make some choices. I'm sorry I've been treating you like a child."

She puts one hand on my cheek and pulls me in to plant a kiss on my forehead.

"Thanks, sis," she says. "Why don't you go take a bath and I'll make dinner?"

"By 'make dinner' do you mean 'order Chinese'?"

She laughs and it feels good to have this moment of levity after the heaviness of this entire day. The Glass Orb has been open for a mere 48 hours. I already feel the weight of this business, coupled with the desire to help Petal figure out her life. I get out of bed and gather up my things for a bubble bath, heading to the kitchen to pour a glass of sweet red wine.

I pour the hot water into the clawfoot tub and undress slowly, surveying my reflection in the mirror. Mascara puddles beneath my eyes and streaks down my cheeks. With a makeup removal wipe, I try to rid my face of the ruined streaks before slipping into the tub. The water encases my body in its gentle wave, and my eyes close against the pleasure of its warmth. While I try to settle into the tub and relax my mind, I can't help but think of a million different things I need to do to get my life back on track.

Step one: I need to get Petal an apartment so that she can get off my couch. Turner already made it clear we weren't going to find a two-bedroom apartment in her budget, especially one that has no security deposit or first and last months' rent. I'm going to need to get creative to help her find a place to live. It would just be a bonus if we could eliminate Turner from the process of finding a place. I'm not sure if I can stomach being around him anymore, not after the mixed messages I keep getting from him. Not with his steady girlfriend in the picture, the one he still has yet to tell me about.

Step two: I need to get The Glass Orb off the ground the right way. As of right now, Petal is the one running this shop. She did almost all of the renovations; she is the one who marketed the place for its soft launch; she is the one who got the *Post and Courier* involved in reviewing us, even if it did fail spectacularly. We need a marketing plan that would get people in the door. I imagine that with a little extra money, I could increase what we're currently paying Petal so that she could afford a two-bedroom apartment. Both of these ideas are tied together. A breakthrough in one area would automatically lead to a breakthrough in the other.

Step three: We need to ace this next review with the *Post and Courier*. The only way we could hope to regain the traction we had on opening day was to give people a reason to see us as reputable. I know we're a sham, but they don't need to. People don't want to waste their money – and I know my clients rarely leave without feeling like they gained at least something small from my reading. I can't imagine which fortune I read on opening day to result in this negative review. In fact, I only remembered reading positive things for the few men who came into the store. The women were a mixed bag, but I remembered men because it was rarer to see them in the context of fortunetelling.

Step four: I need to come up with an exit strategy for myself at The Glass Orb. The truth is that I know I'm not going to be happy here long-term. I never had the vision that I would work as a psychic and fortuneteller for the rest of my life. It was just until something else came along, something viable and more reputable than lying to people all day long. How would I tell Petal that this shop she was so proud of was my worst nightmare come true?

I close my eyes and think over this four-part plan while the bubbles sink over me. I sip the cool wine and relish the way it feels in my throat. The contrast between the ice-cold alcohol and the warm water of the tub feels more delicious than I anticipated. My mind is ping-ponging around the ideas I need to come up with, never settling on any particular solution to the problems I'm facing. Eventually, I grow tired of wrinkled skin. The water cools so I get out and towel off. I slip back into threadbare pajamas, a well-worn pair that always makes me feel better. I can smell the sesame chicken and broccoli in the kitchen and pad down the hall to find Petal plating it for both of us.

"I hope the sesame chicken was okay," she says, passing me a white ceramic plate.

I take it and shovel a bite of the crispy chicken in my mouth, the sweet sauce causing my tastebuds to sing.

"This is perfect," I say, eyes closed as I soak in the flavors. "This didn't come from China Garden though. It's much better than what I usually order there and it's in a different container."

"No, I ordered from Red Jasmine." She crinkles her nose. "China Garden gives us subpar food. It's worth the extra couple of dollars to get something edible."

I have to admit: she has a point. This is perhaps the best sesame chicken I've had in years. The only place I ever order is China Garden because I know what to expect from there. A new place might be even worse. Leave it to Petal to experiment with her takeout and find the ideal place.

"How was your bath?" she asks as we make our way into the living room. I curl up on one end of the sofa bed, my plate balanced on my knees. Petal takes the same posture on her half of the couch, propping herself up with her memory foam pillows. I realize with a start that this posture will soon be nearly impossible for her with her swelling stomach.

"I have a plan," I announce. I outline the first three steps of the plan I came up with in the bath, leaving the fourth step about exiting the business conveniently out of the conversation. Petal still believes this shop could be a dream come true for us; I don't want to shatter the illusion for her while we work to make it profitable. When we're ready, Rose can take over my role of reading fortunes and Petal can run the day-to-day business operations while she paints in her spare time.

We spitball ideas off each other, trying to come up with a marketing plan that would allow us to have a little more cash flow in the business. Petal suggests that we try Facebook marketing, content marketing on a blog about DIY fortunetelling, and workshops where we teach people to read their own tarot cards. I came up with another idea: why not lean heavily into the Glass Orb using a glass orb, the crystal ball that initially got me started with fortunetelling? No one in their right mind believes that crystal balls are something they should base important life decisions on. Maybe this is how we attract new people.

"Why choose just one?" Petal asks, her expression serious.

"You want to do *all* of these ideas?"

"It isn't all that much and it could drum up a lot of business, especially the workshops. If we show people how they can do it themselves, maybe they would be inclined to pay for *different* services when they come see you. No more tarot card readings for you; more answers for them. It's a win-win for everyone."

Petal has a good point. Lots of people wish they understood how to interpret a reading on their own. It was one of the things that I received the most questions about while I was working. The truth is that it would be better for clients if they were to read their own cards. They have intimate knowledge of their personal plight, whatever drove them to seek out our services in the first place. Let them ask their questions and interpret their answers, however they see fit. Plus, it cuts back on the number of people who demand their money back as we saw this morning.

"A workshop," I muse. "How would we advertise that?"

"Leave that to me." Petal's smile causes the skin around her eyes to crinkle and I suddenly think about the girl she used to be. Her face appears much older than it did when she was newly on her own and I was responsible for taking care of her. I don't know how I missed the passage of time, but she's no longer the girl she used to be.

"What about an apartment for you?"

"I have some ideas on that too," she says. "I know I said I didn't want to move in with you. That's still true, but I was thinking maybe I would rent an Airbnb for a little while until Turner can help me find something."

I must wince at the sound of his name because she quickly backpedals.

"I can get a new real estate agent to help me find something. Forget I said anything about him. There are tons of real estate agents in Charleston."

"No, you should use him." I reach out and grab her hand. "You need someone you can trust to help you find the perfect place. Turner is invested in finding something for you," I tell her. "And the baby."

"I really don't have to," Petal says, squeezing my fingers.

"You aren't going to hurt my feelings by using him. We weren't going to get back together. He has a girlfriend, remember?" I try to smile, but I can tell it isn't quite reaching my eyes. Petal seems to sense that I'm not ready to talk about this yet, so she takes another bite of her chicken to buy her time from having to answer.

"I'm really sorry things turned out this way," she finally volunteers.

"Turned out what way?"

"You know what I mean, Essie," she says. "You gave up everything when mom died: your life, your job, your relationship. I know you were just trying to take care of me, but I sent your life on a totally different course. How was I supposed to know you would torpedo your life to take care of me? I wish I had stopped you back then, but I don't think I realized everything you were giving up."

"I would have done it, even if you tried to stop me," I say. Truthfully, I would never have believed that Petal was able to take care of herself. She was always flighty.

"Still, I'm sorry for the part I played in getting us to this point."

"More chicken?" I ask, pushing myself up from the couch and taking her plate.

"I'm ravenous," she says. "I keep waiting for morning sickness to settle in, but the truth is I'm just so hungry all the time."

I head back to the kitchen and scoop more sesame chicken onto the plates. As I'm standing there in my kitchen, it hits me: I can give Petal a chance to raise her baby the right way. She can take my apartment. It might not be two bedrooms, but it has a small sunroom that she could use as the nursery just by putting up a room divider. If she was subletting from me, it would mean that she only needed to cover the rent: no security deposit, no first and last month's rent, no extra fees. I could easily find a new place to live.

The only problem is that I would have to work with Turner to do it.

Chapter 17

"I actually had plans to come by the shop to see you today," Turner says when I call him. "Maybe we can talk about this when I get there this afternoon?"

My heart drops at the thought of seeing him after our last conversation. The wound of what might have been still feels terribly raw, but I need to act quickly to secure a place to live before Petal finds out what my plan is. I swallow hard around the lump in my throat and agree to meet him at the store, as long as he agrees to keep this plan a secret from Petal. I know she would never want me to give up my apartment for her, but it's the only plan that makes sense. I can pay for the security deposit on a new apartment, but the odds are that I won't have to. My credit score is much higher than hers, and most landlords won't require one.

"What do you think about this for the ad copy?" Petal comes out of the office and tosses a piece of paper down on the table. Rose has the day off, so it's just the two of us here, brainstorming what we can do to get more business through the door. I scan the page, but my eyes aren't really seeing it. I never thought I would encourage people to learn how to do this thing that I know isn't even real.

"It needs a better image," I tell her, handing it back to her. What she used was clip art. But if we're going to attract the right kind of people, we're going to need something more than that. I look at the painting on the wall and back to the flyer. "Why don't you paint something for this flyer? You did a beautiful job on the tarot cards you made me. Repurpose some of that art for this."

Petal takes the flyer and studies it while she bites her bottom lip. "Maybe you're right. It could use a little pizazz."

"You might as well put those art skills to good use."

She wanders back to the office with her flyer and I sit there in silence. Nobody comes in to see us. The only other cars in the parking lot are for the Mexican place down the street. I shuffle the tarot cards Petal made me while I watch the parking lot for any sign of life. Eventually, a bright red sedan pops into the parking space right in front of the store. Petal must see the glare of his car, casting a rainbow on the wall. She comes out of the office to take her place at the stand by the door even though I'm more than capable of letting him in.

He comes inside and smiles at Petal while I hide behind the gauzy curtain and take a closer look at him. The guy looks like he must be somewhere in his early thirties, a little soft around the middle but not overweight. Even so, his t-shirt is loose-fitting like he knows that a more form-fit shirt might not be a good idea. At six feet tall, he commands a lot of space in this tiny storefront. I'm so busy surveying him that I miss the entire conversation Petal has with him. They must talk for a couple of minutes before Petal brings him back to my table and gives me a pointed look.

"*Ryan* would like a tarot card reading today," she announces, wiggling her eyebrows when she knows he can't see her.

She's asking me to give him a fake reading so that he can leave satisfied and rewrite that review in the newspaper. Petal has been dancing around this store every time a man comes in, which fortunately few and far between. Maybe if we can get this particular reading over with, I can go back to reading the cards the same way I always do.

"Sit down, sit down," I gesture to the chair across from me. I pass him the deck of cards to shuffle and explain to him how this process will work. It's strange, but I don't remember him being here on the first day we opened. I've seen so many people over the years though. Maybe there wasn't anything particularly memorable about him.

"What questions do you have for the cards today?" I ask, taking the deck back from him. I feel the cards pulse between the palms of my hands, ready for me to pull the top card and ask the question that he came in here for. This reading can't be over soon enough.

"I thought this was always about your love life," he says. "I'm here because a friend told me about you, but I'm not sure if I'm into the whole spiritual practice thing."

"It isn't always about your love life," I explain. "I can only tell you what my intuition has to say about the situation you find yourself in. Why don't you cut the deck, wherever you feel is right, and we'll pull the top card to see what love has in store for you?"

He pulls the deck in half and exposes the top card. I draw in a deep breath before looking down to see what he's drawn.

Death.

Of course, the one person who needs to have a positive fortune to save our store from the brink of utter ruin is the one person who would pull the Death card when he asks about his love life. I glance up at him, trying to think about how to spin the reading so that this comes off in a more positive light. A small smile is tugging at the corners of his lips as if to say that he knows there is absolutely no way I can read something positive.

"The Death card isn't as bad as it might seem," I start, hedging my way around the meaning of the card. "When you pull this card in light of a relationship, it might mean that the relationship you are in is no longer thriving, that some aspect of it has died."

"I'm not in a relationship," he corrects.

"Precisely. This card also means that you might be willing to embrace the changes needed to make a new relationship thrive. A change is imminent for your love life – and that could be for worse or for better depending on the choices you make right now. It means a transformation is on the table for you if you're willing to embrace it."

"I have to say, I didn't think you were going to be able to pull this off," he laughs easily. "I was a skeptic when I came in here, but I saw your sign on the road about answering life's questions. Once I pulled that card, I thought for sure you were going to tell me my relationship was doomed. You have a gift for this."

"Thank you," I tell him, smiling triumphantly. I did it. I impressed the newspaper reviewer. Now, we could drum up a little more traffic for the shop. I hope we are done so I can leave off on a positive note. Instead, I ask, "Is there anything else I can do for you today? A palm reading, perhaps?"

"No, I think that's all I need," he says.

I walk him to the cash register and ring him up for a tarot card reading: the first crisp bills in the cash register today. Before he leaves, he doubles back and stands awkwardly in front of me, wringing his hands.

"I was wondering," he says, looking at the floor as if shy. "Can I get your number?"

I'm taken aback. We just had a conversation about a his dying love life. But then I remember the flip side of the Death card, that it could represent something new for him. Isn't there some kind of line about journalistic integrity when it comes to asking for the phone numbers of the people you're reviewing?

Still, I clock his open expression, the way his eyes dart up to mine as we stand here in silence, watching each other. As I think through my response, it strikes me that this might be the first time a man has asked for my number outside of a dating app or a bar. I'm flattered he thinks enough of me to ask for a phone number, so I scribble my number down on a sticky note.

"Esmerelda," I tell him. "But you should know that I'm here at the store pretty much all the time."

"I'm sure we can work something out." He gives me a little smile and a wave as he walks out the front door. Petal comes rushing onto the main floor as soon as she hears the door chime on his way out.

"Did you *seriously* just give that reporter your phone number?"

"You were the one who told me I should make a good impression on him."

"I didn't mean you should go on a date with him."

"You should have been more specific," I laugh. "It probably won't go anywhere. I'll hold off on going out with him until after he writes the review."

"I wish you would take this seriously."

"I do take it seriously. But you know what else I take seriously?" I point to the Mexican restaurant down the strip. "Lunch."

Petal's hand floats to her stomach and she rubs it for a minute. "Yes, lunch does sound like a good idea for me and baby. Order me a plate of nachos, will you?"

"Can you hold the store down while I run down and get it? I could use a little fresh air and a short break from this place."

Petal nods and eases herself into the chair by the stand in front of the door so that she can quickly spot any new people pulling up. I take a leisurely stroll down to the restaurant, taking my time away from the not-busy store. The hostess takes my order and tells me it will be ready in fifteen minutes, so I decide to wait here for our food. There is a comfortable chair by the front door for me to wait without being in the way of their other customers. I tilt my head back and close my eyes, meditating for a few minutes until she brings me the order.

"Here you go," she says, handing me a white plastic bag with the handles knotted at the top. I thank her and carry it down to the store. I'm greeted by laughter and it takes me by surprise. Petal is sitting in the chair I usually use for readings and she has someone in the chair across from her.

"Petal," I say, surprised to see her with a deck of tarot cards in her hand. "Do you need me to do a reading?"

"No, we were just finishing up," Petal stands and it's then that I notice it isn't just the two women in the store. Turner is sitting on the plastic chairs reserved for waiting clients. She walks over to the register with the woman and takes her money while I turn my attention to Turner. Petal and I can talk about this later.

"Can we go outside and talk?"

He nods and holds the door open for me. Petal is laughing along with the woman inside.

"Do you have any leads on apartments for me?"

"Are you absolutely sure you want to do this without telling her the plan? It kind of seems to go against the whole 'I'm not going to take care of her anymore' thing."

"If I can just get her set up for success and undo some of the damage, I can let her make her own decisions from there."

"I suppose you *could* do that," he says. "I don't have any leads for you yet, but give me a day or two. Maybe Friday we can go see some places, if you can take the morning off?"

"I'll make sure Rose can cover for me."

"All done?" he asks, but his eyes are no longer looking at me.

They're cast just over my shoulder where the woman is walking out of the store. She takes a long look at me, her eyes hard and no smile on her face. I wonder what I've done to make her give me that cold, appraising stare. Then, I put the pieces together. She isn't here for a reading; she is here because she is with Turner and he was coming to see me. This was a very deliberate way for him to let me know there was nothing here between us. His girlfriend nods and walks toward his car in the lot. He walks around to the passenger side door and opens it for her, always the gentleman. It makes me feel sick to my stomach to see him with someone else, but then I remember the small thrill of having someone ask for my number today.

"Since when do you read tarot cards for people?" I ask Petal immediately upon entering the store.

"Relax, Essie," she scolds me. "I was just reading them for Turner's girlfriend. It isn't like she was a serious customer. It was just for fun. Besides, I know the tarot deck just as well as you do. I *made* that tarot deck, remember?"

"Did you catch her name?"

"Actually, no," Petal says, frowning. "I'll have to ask next time they come by."

"I'm hoping there isn't going to be a next time."

"You can't turn away business just because you're hung up on him."

"I wouldn't call it turning away business," I tell her. "And I am *not* hung up on him."

"Whatever you say." Petal dances her way back to the office to keep working on her flyers for the class she's determined we should host. The more I think about it, the more excited I am to get away from this one-on-one reading thing. It's so much pressure to tell someone what they want to hear.

Rose says a good psychic uses everything on the table, meaning we read the people who come across our shop and use the cues they give us to determine how to interpret the cards. Someone who comes in with red-rimmed eyes from crying needs a more uplifting future. Someone who wants to know if love is in the cards for her when she already has a wedding band on her finger needs reassurance. We read exactly what they need at the moment because the cards are so subjective. Teaching people to do this for themselves strikes me as a great way to start on step number four of my plan: moving myself out of the business.

Petal turns on the pop music station on her phone and sings along with it while she paints. Meanwhile, I get a text from an unknown number asking if I would like to have dinner Saturday night. I think about my calendar: open, open, open. I have no reason not to say yes to a date with a handsome, available man even if he happens to be a reviewer for the *Post and Courier*. Maybe I can make a good impression on him over dinner and salvage what's left of our reputation before a new review comes out. I should have asked him when he was going to publish his piece.

I tell him yes not because it's the smart business move but simply because it feels good to be wanted for a change. Turner might be off the table, but that doesn't mean I can't have a decent relationship with someone else.

Chapter 18

"Can you *believe* this?"

Petal is irate, practically screaming with the copy of the newspaper in her hands. It's been two days since Ryan came back to review us again, and Petal's outrage tells me he didn't have anything nice to say. I wonder what he was thinking, writing a negative review and then asking me on a date with him. I make a mental note to cancel the date for Saturday night without telling Petal that I made the arrangement in the first place.

"Listen to this: Esmerelda might be the one who reads your fortune when you come into the store, but it's her sister, Petal, who runs the show. The fortunes you get here are nothing but a sham, I'm sad to report. I wanted to root for this woman-owned business in a part of town that could desperately use revitalization, but alas – save your money and use it on something wiser."

I know from the tone of Petal's voice that this had to be the most scandalous part. I decided right then and there that I wouldn't be reading the rest of the review. Mercifully, it looks short.

"Well, we gave it a fair chance," I tell her. "I *did* read him a great fortune and it wasn't the easiest thing to do."

"I can't believe he would write this," she says.

"You don't know anything about him," I remind her. "And neither do I."

I move away from Petal and walk over to the table with the arrangement of flowers on it. The petals are starting to drop to the tablecloth and the stems are wilting. It's time to toss most of them, but

I can't bring myself to let go of the card. I resolve to slip it into my purse when Petal isn't watching me, and then I'll toss the whole arrangement. Maybe we should invest in fresh flowers for the store more often. Even Chick-fil-A puts fresh flowers on their tables and they're a fast-food restaurant.

"Let's just shut down the store for the night," she says, heading toward the front door to flip off the lights and the open sign. "It's not like we're going to see any customers here the rest of the day. It's been a ghost town and we close in fifteen minutes. I wish I'd seen this article earlier today."

I take the cash drawer out of the register and place the money into the deposit bag. All the while, I'm thinking about Ryan. How is it that the one person who seems genuinely interested in me is also the one person who is out to destroy the entire fragile ecosystem of my four-step plan to improve my life? I shuffle through the closing procedures, thinking all the while about my date the day after tomorrow. Part of me wants to stand him up; part of me knows that I could never be rude enough to do it.

But that doesn't mean I have to pick up the phone and call him.

I pull my phone out of my pocket when Petal isn't around and pull up his number, poising my thumbs over the keyboard. The anger I feel over this bait-and-switch makes it hard for me to think clearly about what I want to say. How dare he come in here and ask me on a date only to write a scathing review about my livelihood. Maybe the entire thing was a joke for him and he intended to stand me up at the restaurant.

Won't make it to our date. Think you know why.

I click send and go back to helping Petal close up. We're wrapping things up when I hear my phone chime. Instead of opening it immediately, I wait until Petal goes into the office to grab her painting supplies. I don't want her to know that I've had any more contact with Ryan. Let her think I was rude enough to stand him up, to make a statement about how I won't be treated like this.

Did you find out about my kinky porn obsession?

I laugh out loud at the missive which draws Petal's unwanted attention. I try to stuff down a smile because I know I can't let myself fall for this guy. Still, I do love his quirky sense of humor.

I know who you are.

I'm just about to lock the front door behind us when my phone chimes again.

That makes one of us. Do you mind letting me know?

Petal casts me a quizzical look. The truth is that I hardly ever pay attention to my phone. Only Petal and Rose text me, and now I hear from Turner occasionally as he hunts for an apartment for me. That last bit isn't something I want to share with Petal though.

I read your piece and I'm not impressed.

I wait until we get home to read the reply: *It's your job to read my cards. You knew that Death was coming for me when you agreed to our date.*

I'm not talking about your cards. I'm talking about your article in the Post and Courier.

I toss the phone onto the kitchen counter, angry with myself for getting sucked into this back-and-forth text message exchange. He made me laugh and he was fairly attractive; did he have to be the one person who was making my job ten times harder? I don't hear anything back from him for a half-hour, at which point Petal and are sitting down on the couch for dinner.

Wow, that's a shitty article.

What am I supposed to make of that? Before I can think too hard about it, my phone chimes again: *But my name isn't Ryan.*

Wait. What?

Petal asked you what your name was and you told her Ryan.

No, I told her my name is Brian. Bryan, if you prefer.

"Petal," I growl at her. "That guy who came by the shop yesterday is *not* named Ryan. Did you not pay attention when you were busy trying to locate our mystery reviewer?"

"What do you mean?"

"His name is *Brian*, with a B."

"Why didn't he correct me when I introduced you to him as Ryan?"

"He must not have noticed. But you almost jeopardized a fairly good chance of having a successful date."

"You're still planning on going out with him?" Petal's eyes are wide and round as if she can't believe I would betray her.

"Why wouldn't I go out with him? He isn't the one who wrote that review."

"I guess you're right," she concedes. "But what if he did?"

"You think he made up a fake name just to write that article and convince me to go on a date with him? Do you realize how paranoid that makes you sound?"

"But then who is Ryan?"

"There were two days' worth of customers that it could have been. I doubt he would give us his real name. As far as journalistic integrity goes, he wouldn't want us to alter our reading based on who he is."

Petal mulls this over while taking a bite of her leftover spaghetti. We eat in silence, the only sound the scraping of our forks against the ceramic plates as we twirl the long noodles.

"Maybe this date could be good for you," Petal finally offers, as if she's giving the date her blessing. "You know, a way to put yourself out there a little bit more."

"I don't have high hopes for it, but he *is* funny."

"What did you read in his cards?"

"Death for his love life. He needs to let go of something to start something new."

"Don't you see?" Petal exclaims and throws a pillow at me. "He has something in his life to let go of and the something new he's starting is with *you*!"

"You don't believe everything you see in the tarot cards, do you?"

"You really can't see how this lines up with your situation? Plus, you're the one who made the reading. You must have had some kind of intuition about what was in his future. Why are you always so down on the cards?"

"Because those cards are just pieces of paper."

"But think about your history with those cards: I gave you a reading before we went to look at the store and look how it turned out. It all came true. Rose gave you a reading and *it* came true, too. Now, you gave *Buh-ryan* a reading and you're starting something new with him."

I shake my head because there's no way Petal can be right about this. These cards don't tell the future. People only think they do because you can twist a reading to mean anything you want it to mean. It's the confirmation bias at work: if you find yourself pulling a card, you will start to think about how it uniquely applies to your life. In other words, you read into the cards what makes the most sense for your situation, no matter what. I explain all of this to Petal who refuses to listen.

"Are you still taking tomorrow morning off?" Petal changes the subject, realizing that it's a dead-end. Neither of us is going to budge on the idea of whether tarot cards really and truly tell the future.

"Rose is going to cover for me, but maybe that isn't necessary," I muse. "You seemed to be pretty comfortable reading those tarot cards for Turner's girlfriend today."

"I can't do what you do." Petal shakes her head, her expression downcast like a puppy who was just told he couldn't get on the sofa. "I'm not sure I have the intuition."

"I bet you could if you practiced a little more. Why don't you read my cards right now?"

"Do you mean it?" Her face brightens and she leaps off the sofa bed and makes her way to the dining room table where it will be easier to lay the cards out. I grab the tarot deck she made for me out of my bag and sit down across from her, shuffling the cards as I go.

"What should we read for you?"

"Why don't you keep it simple? Let's just ask it what my love life is going to hold."

Petal takes a deep breath and closes her eyes to help her focus. I place the deck in front of her and she clears her throat.

"What does your love life hold?" she asks in a clear, ringing voice. She does a great job of setting the mood, making this feel mysterious. Even though I know it's a sham, I'm on the edge of my seat, waiting for her to tell me something I can use to navigate a first date with a guy I hardly know. She pulls the top card off the deck and smiles at it.

"What does it mean?" I prompt her.

"Two of Cups means that a new partnership is on the horizon," she says without thinking. "But I wonder if this is about your love life or our professional life. We need to learn to work in unity just as much as your love life needs a new partner."

"Very good." I break out into a round of applause for her. "You could be a natural at this."

She beams and I collect my cards from her hands, putting them back in my bag.

"Maybe you and Rose should practice tomorrow if you have time. There's no one I would trust more to train you than Rose. It might come in handy to have a third person who can do the heavy lifting around The Glass Orb."

"Do you think I could do it?" Petal asks. Her voice is small and hesitant.

"I do," I confirm. "But I'm going to bed now, so you'll have to practice on your own. You should read the tarot book I keep in the bathroom. It would be a great primer for you on what you need to know."

She practically dances her way to the bathroom to grab the book from its spot beside the tub. She curls up on the sofa bed and dives under the covers, cozy smack dab in the middle of my apartment. I think about how comfortable she is here and smile to myself, knowing that she'll get to stay.

"What are you smiling for?" she asks.

"No reason," I say quickly. "Just happy to see you so excited over something."

"Goodnight, Essie." She rolls her eyes and cracks open the spine of the book to page one. I bid her goodnight and make my way back to the bedroom.

I decide to take a shower before bed so that I can braid my hair, letting it fall in loose waves tomorrow when I have to meet Turner to look at apartments. He always loved my curls. Then, I curse myself for thinking about what I can do to make myself more attractive to him and remind myself that I have a real, live, actual date with a guy who makes me laugh. I take the time in the shower to think about Brian. Brian, who wasn't fazed by my rudeness and who didn't hold my mistake against me. I wondered what it would be like to spend an evening across the table from him, to kiss him goodnight, maybe even to bring him home. Then, I remembered that Petal is sleeping on my couch and I stop thinking about the last item.

Soon, I think. Tomorrow, I will find a great one-bedroom apartment and Petal can have this place to herself.

I flip off the lights and go to sleep, my mind warring between thoughts of Turner and Brian. Part of me wants to move on, to find someone new. The other part of me wants to cling to what feels familiar. Drifting off to sleep, I dream about both of them.

Chapter 19

In the morning, I remember exactly what today holds and jump out of bed. Turner is going to show me apartments, and I want to show him that I'm capable and confident. Then, I remember that I'm doing this because I want to give *my* apartment to Petal, to solve her problem of where to live for her – exactly what he accused me of always doing. He might have a point, but I try not to think about what *he* must think of me. At this point, the only people who should matter to me are Petal and this baby.

I spend a little extra time on my makeup this morning, sweeping on a thin layer of black mascara and smoothing out my foundation for flawless skin. By the time I let the braids out of my hair, I look like someone who is getting ready for a first date more than someone going house-hunting with her ex. I worry that it looks like I've tried too hard and debate taking the makeup off, but Petal is already calling to me down the hall.

"Where are *you* going?" she asks when she sees me.

"I have an appointment today, remember?"

"I'd love to know what kind of appointment you have that warrants all of this." She gestures toward my hair and makeup. "Either way, I'm getting ready to leave for work. I just wanted to let you know I was heading out."

"I'm right behind you," I tell her, grabbing my keys and purse. Turner and I made plans to meet at his office around the same time Petal would be heading to work. This gives us more time to look at apartments without worrying about Petal crossing paths with us.

I slip behind the wheel and put the keys in the ignition, waiting for the car to hum to life. The music is turned up loud, the way I like it when I'm trying to drown out my thoughts. I change the station to rock music, something edgy and angsty to match my current mood. I sing along with every song until I pull up in front of Turner's brick office building in the heart of downtown. He's already waiting for me on the steps that lead up to the office door. When he sees me pull up, he climbs down the steps and slips into the passenger seat of my car.

"You're driving," he says.

"Obviously."

He hands me the address for the first apartment and I punch it into the GPS before we start to drive. I make it two full blocks before Turner says anything to me.

"Are you sure you want to do this?" he asks.

"I don't have other options." I sigh. "Petal needs a place to live that isn't going to cost her an arm and a leg."

"You're taking care of her again," he assesses. "I thought you told me you were going to let her stand on her own two feet."

"This is the last time I'm doing this. She deserves a fresh start for her and the baby. I can't have her sleeping on my couch when she's nine months pregnant. This is as much for me as it is for her."

"If that's what you have to tell yourself."

We pull up in front of a complex of apartment buildings, each one covered in white vinyl siding. There's a small pond at the heart of the community with a fountain in the middle. Even I have to admit that this place looks way swankier than my drab apartment.

"Newly remodeled," he says, noting my assessment of the property. "They just redid these apartments inside and out. I thought you would appreciate that."

We make our way to a second-story apartment with a lockbox on the door. Turner punches in the code, grabs the key from inside, and takes me into what could be my new apartment. I take a deep breath of the new paint smell as I wander in and walk around. The kitchen is fabulous with white and grey marble countertops and white cabinets. Tons of windows let in the natural light, even this early in the morning. The floors are hard surfaces, and I think they look like vinyl even though they resemble hardwood.

"What does this place go for?" I ask Turner when I've made my rounds through every room of the apartment, sadly noting its lack of a clawfoot tub.

"Seventeen hundred," he says without missing a beat.

"I told you my budget was fifteen hundred." I knew this apartment had to be too good to be true. "Why would you waste our time coming here when you knew I couldn't afford it?"

"Two hundred dollars isn't so far out of your budget. Maybe you do a couple more readings a month and you can afford a place like this. It's *aspirational*," he emphasizes.

"In case you didn't know, we're having a little publicity problem at the moment."

He looks around and I notice that he isn't meeting my eye.

"Admit it," I say. "You don't think Petal can pull this off."

"It's not that," he says. "Maybe we should move on to the next apartment if this one isn't the one for you."

We leave the apartment and he locks up behind us. We ride in silence to the next place, a building that seems more like something that aligns with my budget. It's older but still in livable shape. The cabinet fronts are peeling at the corners and there is old shag carpeting throughout the main living areas, but there's a great eat-in kitchen, it gets tons of natural light, and it doesn't smell too horrible for having age-old carpet.

"Sixteen hundred," Turner says.

Shit. Even this place is out of my budget.

"Did you find *any* apartments that were within my budget or is this your way of collecting higher commission?"

"I'm not going to charge you a commission on finding an apartment, Ess." I can practically hear the eye roll in his voice. "The market is hot right now. Fifteen hundred is too low to find a place that's in a good part of town."

"Well, I have to say: if the difference between this place and the other is only a hundred bucks, I would much rather have the other one."

"Does that mean you want to sign a lease there?"

I sigh and nod. It's better to get this over with as quickly as possible, figuring out exactly how much this move is going to cost me in security deposits and the first month's rent. As we make our way back to the first property, I start to do some mental math on my bank account and realize that I'm dwindling it down to almost nothing. At least I never bought that mattress when Mark and I were together. I'll have to hope that Brian is a gentleman tomorrow and pays for dinner.

"Hi, Lacie," Turner greets the chirpy blonde at the front counter of the leasing office at the apartment complex. "I have a client who's interested in 2H. Can you help us out?"

"We've had a lot of interest in that apartment," she muses. "Must be the remodeling. I knew that would be good for business."

"I think she's ready to sign a lease if you can pull one up for us." Turner looks at me to confirm and I nod at Lacie.

"I'm sorry," Lacie says. "I should have introduced myself. I'm Lacie. You'll find me here during normal business hours during the week if you ever need anything."

"Esmerelda," I say, offering her my hand. Her skin feels smooth and warm in mine.

"What a unique name," she muses, already tapping away on the keyboard of her computer.

"It's even better when you learn what she does for a living," Turner says. "She's a psychic."

Lacie stops typing and looks up at me, really examining me for the first time. "You speak to spirits?"

"I'm not a medium," I correct her. It's a common misconception when people hear what I do for a living. "I read the future, mainly tarot cards but I do some palm reading too."

Lacie looks disappointed.

"My aunt recently crossed over. I've been dying to ask her questions about what it was like and about what happened to her," she muses. "Maybe you know a medium?"

"Nope," I tell her. "I don't know anyone."

She sighs and continues to peck at her keyboard. The three of us sit there in awkward quiet while she works on the paperwork. Things never really improve, but she does collect my money: no security deposit due to my stellar credit, a $200 administrative fee, and the pro-rated portion of the first month's rent at $760. Altogether, I fork over $960 and breathe a sigh of relief that I still have almost $50 in the bank. We finish our transaction and she hands me a set of keys to both the apartment and the mailbox.

"Welcome to Water's Edge," she says as we're leaving.

"I bet that was the fastest you've ever leased an apartment," I tease Turner when we get in the car. "Now, you can get back to the paying customers."

"Do you want to grab lunch with me first? I'm starving."

My heart flutters at the idea of spending more time with him, even though I know I should make an excuse not to go with him. We are already in the car and driving back toward downtown, so it only makes sense to go to Jestine's for brunch. My mouth waters at the idea of chocolate chip pancakes slathered with butter and syrup, crispy bacon, and a hot cup of coffee with her homemade coconut milk creamer.

"Turner and Essie," she greets us when we walk through the door. "I always knew I would see the two of you back here again."

I cringe and my face heats up as Turner rushes to tell Jestine that we are here together, but we aren't together, together. She laughs and brushes it off.

"Is Petal joining you today too?"

"Just us," I tell her.

"I'll give you two a more *private* table." She winks and gestures for us to follow her to the back room where only a handful of people are seated. We slide into a table made for two in front of the window looking out onto the city street. "I'll get you two some coffee to get started."

Turner and I sit awkwardly across from each other, both of us focusing on the menu when we already know that we'll order the same things we always do. Jestine mistaking us for being a couple again really throws me for a loop, maybe because I wish it were true. Then, I remember that he already has a girlfriend and so I draw my attention to that fact. He doesn't need to know that I might be hung up. I can be happy for him and his new relationship.

"Your girlfriend seems nice," I finally say. He winces and looks up at me.

"We don't have to do this."

"Do what?" I widen my eyes to look innocent. "I thought you two seemed great together."

"I know we have a history, so we don't need to talk about our personal lives."

"We've both moved on," I inform him, a small smile on my lips because I know that I at least have something positive to report in this department. "I have a date tomorrow night, and it could be very, very promising. There's no reason we can't talk about these things. After all, we used to be close friends."

"If you're sure this is what you want to do," he says and hesitates. "I'm glad you think we seem good together because it's kind of a permanent thing."

"What do you mean – a permanent thing?" I glance down, but there's no wedding band on his finger. That's something I'm sure I would have seen.

"We're engaged," he says, his face turning the lightest shade of pink. "The wedding is in five months."

"I can't believe I didn't notice the ring on her hand," I muse, but inwardly I can feel betrayal deep in my gut. Here we are together, for the first time in years, eating pancakes and drinking coffee and talking about our lives. Only, he seems to have moved on with his life while I'm still going on first dates with random guys I meet at work.

"You weren't the one who read her cards," he explains. I would have to tell Petal to pay more attention to *everything* on the table when she reads cards from now on. "I don't think Petal noticed. She was having too much fun playing the psychic."

"I hope she was happy with her fortune," I tell him. "Petal is going to start trying to learn how to do it too. Rose and I are going to teach her."

"Ryan was pretty impressed with her." He shrugs.

I feel the weight of his words in my stomach, and it feels like the bottom has dropped out with that one sentence.

"Your fiancée's name is *Ryan*?"

He nods and looks down at his coffee.

"I have to go," I tell him, standing up and throwing the chair back. "I can't believe you would let her write those pieces about our shop and pretend like you didn't know anything about it."

"Ess, sit down."

"Why? So you can sit across from me and lie to me about your love life and why your fiancée suddenly has it out for me?"

"Sit," he commands. "I'll explain."

"I'll stand, but this better be one hell of an explanation."

"She took the assignment because she knew it would be a huge favor to me if she reviewed your store positively. Despite what you may think, I still consider you and Petal to be close friends. We were together for years, Ess." He sighs. "But then she came to get her reading and saw the sunflowers I sent you on the table with the note. She got jealous and accused me of wanting her to write the piece because I still had feelings for you."

"This is seriously all your fault," I summarize. "If you hadn't convinced her to take the job. If you hadn't sent me flowers. We could have had a great review *and* some traffic to the store."

"I suppose you could look at it that way," he says, miserable.

"I don't know any other way to look at it. You need to get things straight with *Ryan* and try not to ruin anything else in my life, if possible."

I walk out of the restaurant and get in my car before I remember that I drove him here. The office is only a few blocks away or he can take an Uber. What has he done to make *my* life more convenient lately? Convince me to rent an apartment that's two hundred dollars out of my price range?

I drive straight to the store and walk in on Rose and Petal practicing reading tarot cards in the corner.

"We need to talk about this review in the paper," I tell her.

"Can it wait until we're done with this session?"

"No, it cannot."

Petal stands up from the table and looks at Rose apologetically. Rose shrugs and starts to stack the cards back into a pile from the seven-card spread laid out on the table in front of her. We walk back to the office and shut the door behind us so that no customers can hear us if they walk in. Rose has the store under control, and I'll clue her into what's going on later.

"Do you want to know who *Ryan* is?" I hiss at her.

"Of course, I do." Petal shakes her head. "Is that what you've been doing this morning? Playing detective?"

"I didn't have to play detective because the answer came right to me. Ryan is Turner's fiancée."

"Fiancée?" she asks in a small voice.

"Fiancée," I confirm. "Apparently, you didn't notice the ring on her hand and she wasn't exactly eager to give us her name and ruin the façade of coming in just for a reading. She saw the flowers on the table and the note from Turner, assumed there was something going on between us, and wrote a scathing review."

"Ouch," Petal murmurs, her hand absentmindedly wandering to the newspaper on the desk. "What are we supposed to do to fix this?"

"I don't know what the solution is," I tell her. "But there must be *something* we can do to keep her from destroying this shop. Maybe we could write an op-ed for the newspaper about her journalistic integrity?"

"I doubt anyone is going to read that and decide to come visit our store."

"Well, we have to do *something*."

"Maybe we should just keep course. Teach the class, pay for ads, and keep offering services to walk-ins. Eventually, everyone will forget about the review."

"That's a much different mindset than you had a few days ago," I remind her. "Back when it was my fault we had a negative review."

"I don't see how we're going to convince her that there's nothing going on between you two, especially when you sneak off with him like you did this morning."

My mouth falls open. I know I didn't tell her that.

"Look at you," she says, gesturing to my hair and makeup. "Who else would you dress up for like this?"

"Even if you were right," I bite each word off carefully, "I might have a reason for getting together with him without telling you."

"Why don't we continue this conversation at home?" Petal asks. "Take the rest of the day off and let Rose watch the store."

Chapter 20

"What were you thinking?" Petal explodes when we walk through the front door. I'm glad we drove separate cars to the store this morning so I had a few minutes to calm down and collect my thoughts before we got here. "She has it out for us, Esmerelda. You have to make this right."

"What do you want me to do? Head to her house and convince her that nothing is going on between me and her fiancée?" I laugh at the idea of showing up on her doorstep, trying to tell her that I know things look suspicious, but there really, truly is nothing going on between us. Maybe this morning it would have been hard for me to admit that, but now? Things are definitely, totally, and completely done between us – no matter what I might have thought was there before. Tears prick the back of my eyes as I think about what I gained only to lose it again.

"It would be a good starting point," Petal argues, breaking me out of my reverie. "But maybe you should take off the makeup and throw on some old clothes first."

"I have every right to dress however I want."

"But do you have to be so *obvious* about what you want?"

"And what is it that you think I want, Petal?"

"It's obvious that you want to get back together with him. The way you look at him, the way you light up when he touches you, the way you stare at that flower arrangement he sent you, trying to figure out what it all means," she says. "I should have never called him."

"You're right," I concede bitterly. "You shouldn't have called him. In fact, we wouldn't be in this situation right now if it weren't for your impulsive decision to start The Glass Orb. I could be a secretary or doing something that *matters*. Instead, I'm sitting in this shop and pretending to tell the future."

"So you wish I had never tried to help you build a real future for yourself?"

"I wish you had at least consulted with me before you made another decision that would affect both of us for years to come." I shake my head and turn my back to her so that I can walk to the kitchen. I need a glass of wine. "But that seems to be your habit these days – making decisions that can't be undone and hoping everyone else goes along with them."

"What is that supposed to mean?"

"You opened this shop and hoped I would come along with you, and you never asked me. You decided to have this baby and hoped Jason would go along with it, even though he *told* you it wasn't the future he wanted."

As soon as I say the words out loud, I regret them.

"Petal—"

"No," she interrupts me. "You're right. I should have consulted you before I turned both our lives upside down. You were going to be out of a job and I knew you would never pursue what actually mattered to you. So, I opened this shop and tried to give you a better future." She takes a deep breath. "Jason told me he didn't want kids, but I knew he would make a great dad. Finding out I was pregnant was good news for me, but not so much for him. I wasn't careful."

"Maybe I would have landed on my feet," I tell her. "Maybe I would have pursued a career that actually made me happy. But we're kind of stuck with this shop now. I'm sorry for what I said about Jason. It wasn't fair of me."

"You always go along with what other people want for you," she says. "And I guess I've gotten used to being the one who has to make the decisions."

I laugh, thinking about the events of the day. It seemed like another lifetime when Turner and I were signing the lease on a new apartment so I could give this one to Petal. Once again, I was not only disrupting my life to take care of her, but I was also going along with what she wanted for herself and for me.

"Actually, I made a decision for me today," I tell her. "I'm moving."

She opens her mouth and looks around the apartment, obviously wondering where she is going to go with her boxes and her sofa bed. "But you love this apartment."

"I do." I pause for a minute and let that sink in for her. "But I know you do too. I'm going to sublet it to you when I move: no security deposit, no first and last month's rent. Look. You can put up a room divider here and let this be the nursery. You'll want to hang some blackout curtains to keep it dark so the baby can sleep, but it's the perfect nursery space."

"I feel like a huge bitch," she finally says and I laugh. "You're completely turning your life upside down for me to have what I want. You deserve to do something for yourself."

"Petal, you're my little sister. I've always taken care of you. I can't let you give birth while you sleep on my sofa."

"But you're giving up this apartment and you're working a job you hate. Where does that leave you?"

"I guess it means I need to start over."

"What does that mean?"

I take a deep breath and make my way over to the sofa with my glass of wine. I curl up on the corner of the sofa bed and take a sip of the sweet red. Petal comes to curl up beside me and it almost feels like the anger that flared up when we sat down no longer exists between us. She is soft and tender, feeling every tendril of my emotion. Petal has always been good at soaking up the emotions of others.

"I think I need a fresh start," I tell her. "A new job, a new career, a new love life."

"Don't you love your life here in Charleston?"

"Petal, I love *you* but I'm not so sure there's anything here for me anymore besides you and this soon-to-be baby."

"It's a girl," she blurts out. "I found out this morning."

"A girl," I muse, thinking about the sisterhood we would be welcoming her into. "A healthy, beautiful baby girl."

"Don't you want to be around when she's born?"

"Who says that I won't be?" I shrug. "I think I just need some time to pursue a life that I create for myself, nobody else. I need to break free of this pattern I'm in where I solve everyone's problems and never do what makes me happy."

"What does it look like for you to be happy?"

"To start, I think it means I'm done telling fortunes. Petal, you can do it just as well as I can with a little practice. Plus, you have Rose who taught me how to do it and she can do the same for you. You've always been *interested* in this and it's flexible enough for you to paint and work at the same time."

"But what will you do?"

"I don't know," I tell her. "Maybe I'll go back to school and get a real, grown-up job."

"Is this all because of Turner?"

I sigh and shake my head. "It certainly doesn't help. You brought him back into my life and I thought that was what I wanted, but there's too much history between us. He would never be able to see me as anyone but the girl I was back when we were together. History repeats itself."

"It was shitty of him not to tell you he was engaged," Petal says, indignant on my behalf. "I can't believe he never mentioned it in any of the conversations we had while I was looking for a commercial lease."

"It doesn't matter," I tell her, realizing the truth as I say it. "He wanted to flirt with the idea of us getting back together. It's comfortable and familiar. But he has a life that's separate from mine now. That's the way it should be."

"I'm sorry things turned out this way, Essie." Petal wipes a tear from the corner of her eye and laughs. "Pregnancy hormones."

"I think we need to make a plan for how the rest of this year is going to play out." I reach over and take her hand. "I really don't think I can keep working at The Glass Orb with you. This needs to be your thing. I'm only muddying the waters. You can probably get a great review from Ryan if she knows I'm no longer in the picture at the shop."

"You really don't want to come back to work with me?" Petal sticks out her lower lip. "Is it really so bad to spend all of that time with me?"

"It isn't that I don't want to work with you," I tell her. "It's that I don't want to do *this* work with you. I'm tired of pretending about everything in my life. I feel like I never have the chance to be honest with myself or anyone else."

"Don't come back," Petal says, nodding enthusiastically. "If this is really how you feel, I don't want you to jeopardize your future. Rose and I will make it work. I'll hire someone else if I need to, and let Rose train them. Take some time off and see where your soul-searching leads you. Do you want me to pull a tarot card for you?"

I groan.

"Haven't you been listening to anything I'm saying? I hate this whole idea that we can tell the future. I most certainly do *not* want you to read my cards."

Petal pouts and I almost give in to her before remembering that I'm turning over a new leaf. I'm no longer going to cave to anyone else's demands. I'm going to live life on my own terms, and that has to start right now. If I cave immediately, I'll never stand on my own two feet to secure a future where I can be happy.

"Fine," she says, realizing I won't give in. "But what are we going to do about your living situation?"

"I'm going to move to this new apartment," I tell her. "I'll be close enough to help out with the baby some when she's born, but we'll have separation. I can find another job locally and think about what I want to do long-term."

"If you're sure that this is what you want," she says. "I have to say this worked out for me. Can we go see your new apartment?"

"I don't think so," I laugh. "It's so much nicer than this place that you'll want to trade with me."

"But I bet it doesn't have that clawfoot tub," she says.

Petal and I laugh together and she nestles into my side, resting her head in the crook of my neck. She feels warm against me. Everything is right in the world for a change. She is still here, she is still my sister, and we no longer have to work together and live together. We can go to Jestine's for pancakes on Sunday mornings while everyone else is in church, and we can enjoy each other's company without it torpedoing both of our lives. It feels good to have a plan.

Chapter 21

The next morning, I wake up to the sunlight streaming in my window. I roll over and realize that my alarm clock reads 9:30 A.M. and I jump out of bed, forgetting for a moment that I have nowhere else to be today. Petal and I agreed last night that my tenure at The Glass Orb was officially over as of today until I decide what I want to do. Today is reserved for soul-searching, moving, and a first date. After Petal and I argued yesterday, it seemed like my entire life fell into place. I was getting a new place to live, a new job, and a new love life all in one fell swoop.

Because it's so late, Petal is already gone for work. I don't have to worry about her overhearing me sing in the shower, so I turned the music up loud and let the warm water run over my back. After I finish showering, I decide to take the time to actually do my hair for a change. I want to make a good impression on Ryan. *Brian*, I correct myself. I spend some time under the heat of my hairdryer and curling iron until I'm pleased with the end result. I know the curls won't still be as big and voluminous eight hours from now when we go to dinner, but it will still lend my hair some wave and body.

Petal left me a few cups of coffee in the coffee pot alongside a note that told me it was my favorite local coffee blend. She wished me luck finding something to do with my day. I take another luxurious deep breath, realizing that there's nowhere and nothing I need to do until my date with Brian. I pour the coffee, add a splash of creamer, and sit down on the couch which Petal folded back into a sofa with her blankets neatly folded on the armchair. It feels like I finally have my house –

and my life – back. I can feel myself standing on the cusp of a new beginning, but then I realize I have almost no safety net. My savings account is going to be eaten up with the move to a new apartment: renting a truck, hiring movers, and taking time off work all are going to cost me financially.

The question is: what exactly do I want to do with my life if I'm not going to be reading the future for desperate people?

There really seems to be only one answer if I want a job that will not only pay the bills but make me want to actually go to work in the morning. I'm not going to find that at a temp agency. I won't be lucky enough to stumble into something like I did with Rose, and I have no education to back up my skills and experience. Fortuneteller doesn't look so great on a resume when applying for a professional job. I might as well list "professional scam artist" as my previous employment, even if I was successful enough to think about launching my own shop.

I pull out my laptop and navigate to the local community college page to browse through the list of academic programs. The list is significantly longer than I thought it would be, covering everything from women's and gender studies to accounting. It seems that any career I might want to pursue is available to me for the low price of $6,000 per semester. I silently thank the heavens that I'm a resident because the tuition is almost double that for out-of-state students. I will have to pick something from this list if I want to get a real job, but what's the right fit for me?

After a couple of hours of perusing the website, I'm still no closer to determining what it is I should do with my one wild and precious life. I set the laptop aside and get up to pour myself a second cup of coffee. As I open the refrigerator door, I realize the only things I have in here are takeout containers. Petal and I have been so busy since the store opened and I had to go apartment hunting that I haven't had a chance to go grocery shopping. With a sigh, I transfer my coffee into a travel mug and grab my purse and keys. Even though this isn't exactly how I would have pictured spending my day, it can't be any worse than sitting in The Glass Orb waiting for someone to come along and tell me I'm nothing more than a fraud.

I'm halfway through the grocery store with a cart full of produce when I hear someone call out my name. I wince because there is no way to avoid the fact they mean me. I wish I had a less distinct name like Taylor or Brittany where I could pretend that they didn't mean for me to turn around. With a sigh, I turn around and look for whoever called my name. At the end of the aisle is a man waving to me, a little soft around the middle. *Brian*, I think to myself.

"Fancy meeting you here," he says, bringing his cart closer to mine. I'm glad I took the time this morning to do my hair and makeup. He strikes me as more attractive than I remember, but maybe it's because I'm no longer hung up on Turner. That chapter of my life is officially over and done with.

"Brian," I laugh out of the sheer delight of running into him here. "I can't believe we ran into each other here when we have a date tonight. If I didn't know better, I would say that maybe you're following me around."

"You have the day off today?"

"Something like that," I muse, thinking about how I technically have every day off from here on out. I don't want it to sound like I got fired from my job and I don't want to come across as flighty for quitting without a solid backup plan. "What are you up to today that you can come to the grocery store in the middle of the day?"

"I have off," he says. "Perks of a four-day work week. Say, do you want to get lunch instead of dinner since we're already out here?"

I look at my cart, heaped full of produce. "I would love that, but I need to get groceries. There's nothing in my house except Chinese takeout containers. Can we meet up in a half-hour after I pay and unload these?"

He looks down at his cart which is stacked high with cereal boxes and cartons of orange juice. I notice that he has a box of cotton candy Go-Gurt in the bottom of his basket and I reach out and grab it. "Please tell me this is for a child and not for you."

"I have the palate of a child, unfortunately," he laughs.

"Maybe you just haven't been exposed to the right adult foods," I surmise, looking at all of the processed food in his cart. "Why don't I make us lunch and you can meet me at my place in a half hour?"

"Can I bring my own box of mac and cheese in case I don't like what you're serving?"

I laugh and nod. "Bring whatever you want to contribute to the meal. I'm going to go pick up a few things to expand your tastebuds a little bit, but then I'll check out and head home. Finish your shopping and just text me when you're on your way."

He jots down my address and we part ways with a friendly wave. I circle back to produce, grabbing some asparagus and red pepper. I pick up a can of black beans and some mozzarella cheese, tortillas and mango salsa. I'm going to make primavera quesadillas for him, loaded with the healthiest vegetables I can find. This seems like a nice segue from his processed garbage to a more substantial meal with actual nutritional value. With my ingredients in the cart, I run through the self-checkout, bag my groceries, and dart home. When I walk through the door, I'm grateful Petal has cleaned up the place a little bit so he doesn't realize my sister is sleeping on the sofa.

I put away the groceries in a hurry and run to the bathroom to make sure it's clean enough to have a guest over. I throw new hand towels on the rack, refill the soap dispenser, and run an anti-bacterial wipe over the sink to clear away the loose hair and toothpaste in the ceramic bowl. I sit on the barstool that lines the kitchen and wonder what we're going to talk about when he gets here. My relationship with my ex whose fiancée is sabotaging my store that is no longer my store, but actually my pregnant sister's store? Maybe it was a mistake to invite

Brian over instead of sticking with our dinner date. All I know is that when I saw him, I didn't want to wait to have dinner with him.

I'm mulling over how to explain my life in polite conversation when he knocks on the door. I glance down at my phone and realize he texted me fifteen minutes ago that he was on his way. It never chimed because I still had it on silent overnight. I have gotten out of the habit of turning the ringer on because I never want it to interfere with a reading. Plus, Petal lives here now so there's no way she's going to call me in an emergency. Damn. I could have used those fifteen minutes to prepare myself.

Instead, I take a deep breath and open the front door. Brian stands on the other side of the threshold, and I notice that he's wearing a new t-shirt and holding a small bouquet of wildflowers. When he sees me, a smile lights up his whole face. This is what I've been missing, hung up on Turner all this time. I could have had someone who was *thrilled* to see me instead of someone who would lie about their engagement by omission.

"You changed your outfit," I accuse him playfully.

"Well, yeah," he says, blushing a little bit. "I wanted to look nice for our date."

"It looks nice on you. The green suits you. Come in, come in," I tell him, walking down the hall to the kitchen. "I was thinking about making quesadillas for us. How does that sound?"

"I love a good quesadilla," he smiles.

"These are going to be *grown-up* quesadillas. We're going to expand your palate."

He sits down at the bar I just vacated and watches me start assembling the basic ingredients of our lunch. I start grating mozzarella cheese that will hold everything together while the oven preheats to cook the asparagus.

"Is there anything I can help with?"

"If you want to prep the asparagus, I wouldn't complain," I offer, pointing to the bushel of asparagus next to me on the kitchen counter. I look up to see him hesitate at the threshold of the kitchen, wringing his hands. "You don't know how to prep asparagus, do you?"

"Admittedly, no," he says, bashful. "But I'm a quick learner."

I show him how to snap off the woody ends, give him instructions to drizzle it with extra-virgin olive oil, and sprinkle it with salt and pepper before fanning it out on a cooking sheet. He takes to his task seriously and I watch him out of the corner of my eye while I grate the cheese. Seeing a man in my kitchen making asparagus is more appealing than I thought. Turner never helped me cook. I shake my head. He isn't what I want to think about while I'm standing here on a date with someone new.

"Is everything okay?" Brian asks, noticing my head shake.

"Yeah," I smile up at him. "I was just thinking that today isn't turning out the way I would have pictured it a week ago."

"What's different about today than you thought?"

"Well, I was supposed to work today," I offer, not sure how much I want to tell him about my personal life. Brian seems sweet and thoughtful, and I don't want to lie. It seems the best thing I can do is tell the truth. If this is going to go anywhere, I can't lie about the fact that I do not, at present, have a job.

"And then you got the day off?"

"More like I got *every* day off," I amend. "I quit."

"But you own the store," he says, confused. I love the way his brow furrows and the corners of his mouth drag down when he isn't sure what's going on.

"Technically, my sister owns the store."

"The girl with the short hair who greeted me when I came in?"

"Petal," I nod. "She leased the storefront because she thought I might want to strike out on my own and start a business with her. It was a surprise for me, but it turns out that fortunetelling just isn't the right fit."

"You were really good at it, you know," he says. "You were spot on with my reading. If it weren't for that reading, I doubt I would be standing here making asparagus."

"I might have been good at it, but it's a sham. There's no such thing as telling the future." I sigh. "The cards are so subjective that anyone can read into anything I pull for them. That's the beauty of fortunetelling: everyone gets the message they most want to hear. I hate taking money from people for something that isn't strictly true."

He continues to snap asparagus stems while he thinks this over for a minute.

"That makes sense," he says. "You want to earn an honest living. I don't think anyone can fault you for that. But what will you do now if you don't want to read tarot cards for a living?"

I put away the cheese grater and start sprinkling the cheese over the tortillas while Brian slides the cooking sheet into the oven for ten minutes. This is the conversation I'm not sure I want to have with him, and yet here we are. Maybe this could be a good thing: starting a potential relationship with honesty instead of the lies I fed him when he came into The Glass Orb.

"I'm honestly not sure," I finally say. "I was thinking about going back to school, getting my degree in something so that I can get a real job. One with benefits and a salary."

He nods, thoughtful for a moment. "What do you like to do?"

"What do I like to do?" I muse, a question I've been asking myself all morning as I browsed the college course catalog. "You know, I've spent so long trying to make sure everyone around me is happy and taken care of that I think I got a little lost along the way." I realize after I say it that I didn't intend to be this honest with him. For a first date, we are heading into dangerous territory, but Brian seems unfazed by it.

"And one of the people you try to take care of is your sister," he guesses.

"She's the primary person I try to take care of," I explain. "She's my little sister, four years younger than I am. When our mom died, she had a really hard time coping because she was just starting her adult life. I guess ever since then, I've had a hard time letting her learn life lessons on her own."

"But that means you have no idea what you would choose to do if the opportunity presented itself – which it has."

"That's exactly right." I light up at his understanding. I can feel the way my smile stretches across my cheeks to be understood this way by someone. It feels like this is more like our fifth or sixth date instead of an impromptu first date in my kitchen.

"Maybe we should find out what you like to do," he says, climbing back on the barstool while I keep prepping the quesadillas. "Let's set you up with a personality test to see what you could explore. Where's your computer?"

I point in the direction of the living room where I left it on the couch that morning. He grabs it and brings it back to the bar, punching away at the keys as he searches for what he wants. I realize as he's typing that we've spent this whole conversation talking about me and I don't even know what he does for a living, so I ask.

"Psychologist," he says with a laugh. "Maybe I should have led with that. It's why I like to listen to other people's stories and solve their problems. Maybe it's my character defect."

"You certainly are good at it," I tell him, smiling. How could I possibly be standing here with a guy who seems perfect on paper when just yesterday I found out my ex has a fiancée and I thought my whole world was going to come crumbling down?

"Alright, are you ready for the first question?"

"Shoot," I tell him as I turn around to grab the asparagus from the oven. He takes a deep breath and reads the first question, then the second. We spend twenty minutes going over an intense personality survey while I grill quesadillas on the cooktop. It feels nice to think about what I like and want to do, but I admit it feels nicer to have someone listen and understand what I need.

"The test doesn't tell you what you should do for a living," Brian prefaces my results. "But it does give you some areas of interest to consider."

"And what would those areas of interest be?"

"It says here you have an analytical mind, which makes sense given your current position. You use everything that people show you to come up with a reading that's tailored to them. You may not be a true psychic if that even exists, but you're great at reading people." He scrolls through the results a little bit further. "You also scored high in empathy which means you're great at relating to people."

"This sounds like I should just keep my day job." I turn back to the cooktop to remove the quesadillas. "Maybe this is what I'm good at and I should just stick to it."

"Not necessarily," he says. "You might have just internalized the skills required to be good at your day job. Now, they come as second nature to you. There are tons of job opportunities out there that could match up with your skills."

"Name three."

"Well, the first one that comes to mind is counseling. You're good at reading people and you know how to relate to people, to give them what they need. If you wanted to press into the more analytical aspects of your personality, you could be a paralegal or an accountant." He pauses to collect his thoughts for a minute. "I don't think there's necessarily one right answer here. Your skills could come in handy in almost any job."

I pass him a plate with his quesadilla on it and a dollop of mango salsa for dipping. I climb up on the barstool next to him, and I feel the electricity that passes between us as my arm brushes against his. This is the best afternoon I've spent in quite some time, even better than my time with Turner *before* I knew he was engaged. When was the last time someone genuinely listened to what I was going through and helped me problem-solve?

Brian takes a small nibble off the triangular point of his quesadilla slice, skipping the salsa dipping.

"The salsa is what makes these quesadillas stand out," I scold him.

He makes a big show of dipping his quesadilla into the chunky salsa and taking a big bite. I laugh at his surprised face as he chews, clearly not expecting to enjoy the meal I made for him.

"It's good, right?" I say, taking a bite of my own quesadilla. It's been ages since I made a real meal, something healthy and satisfying. Ever since Petal moved in, we've been going along with her cravings which usually means lots of takeout – fried foods, junk food, basically any food except for a vegetable.

"I have to admit, this is better than I thought it would be. Maybe I actually *like* asparagus."

"I'm glad I could open up your tastes like you opened up my field of career possibilities." I laugh as he continues to eat his quesadilla carefully. "Really and truly, this has been a great afternoon and I appreciate your help trying to figure out what I should do next."

"All I did was help you take an online quiz." He shrugs.

"But I would have never thought about those possibilities. I know it doesn't make decisions for me, but it was helpful to have a new perspective from someone who doesn't really know me."

"I'd like to get to know you." Brian blushes and looks down at his plate.

I open my mouth to respond to him in kind because I need to see where this thing is going, but the front door cracks open. Petal walks through the door, calling out, "Honey, I'm home!" When she makes it down the hallway and sees us sitting at the bar, she backpedals for a minute.

"I'm sorry, Essie," she says, doubling back toward the front door. She looks embarrassed to have interrupted us. "I didn't know you had company. I can go run some errands."

"Please don't leave on my account," Brian says. "I believe I owe you an apology."

"You owe me an apology? Did you steal my favorite sweater?" She laughs.

"It seems there was some kind of mix-up at the store where you thought my name might have been *Ryan* and I didn't correct you." He looks sideways at me. "But I'm glad you did because otherwise, I might not be sitting here on one of the best dates I've had in a long time."

Petal looks at me and raises her eyebrows. I drop my gaze to the empty plate in front of me as the flush settles over my cheeks. The truth is that I've had just as good a time as Brian did, and that scares me a little bit.

"I should get going," Brian says, stacking his plate on mine and taking them to the kitchen sink.

"I'll be in the bathroom getting a shower," Petal says in an attempt to make herself scarce. She disappears down the hall and slips into the bathroom, making a big show of closing the door behind her. I don't say anything to Brian until I hear the water turn on, certain that she isn't going to come out and surprise us.

"I did have a great time with you this afternoon," I tell him as I walk him to the front door. "And I'm glad my cooking didn't scare you off."

"I'd like to do this again." He looks me in the eye and brushes a hand along my cheekbone, a mirror of the way Turner touched me on that first dinner. Yet, it feels different. "Soon."

I nod, unsure what's going to come next. The warmth where he brushes against me is pleasant. This isn't the way I felt with Mark, the mattress salesman who left me after saying that we weren't exclusive. That was just comfortable and barely desirable. This is heat, desire.

Slowly, he leans in toward me and I close my eyes because I know I might panic if I have to watch him come in close. He brushes his lips against mine once, twice. My body curls in toward him as if it had a mind of its own. I wish Petal wasn't home so that we could explore this further, but he pulls away with a little chuckle.

"We have time," he says, tucking a strand of hair behind my ear. "I'll text you?"

"Please," I say, opening the door to let him out. As soon as he's gone, I lean up against the doorframe and breathe a sigh of relief. It turns out I *am* capable of having a new relationship, one that isn't as dysfunctional as my past with Turner. He doesn't have to know who I used to be, and we can move forward based on who I am right now: independent, adventurous, and uncertain about what the future might bring.

I float to the sofa and curl up in the corner with my phone to scroll through social media, just until I hear the shower stop running. I have a feeling Petal wasn't taking an actual shower but merely using it as an excuse to give us some privacy. For once, I'm glad she didn't take me up on the offer to move in with her. I want the freedom to explore where this could go with Brian.

"I thought your date wasn't until tonight," she accuses me when she prances out of the bathroom, fully dressed and dry.

"We ran into each other at the grocery store and modified our plans."

"How was it?" She climbs on the other end of the sofa and tucks her knees into her chest. "It seemed like you were having a good time."

"We were." I smile and feel the blush rise in my cheeks. "It was the best date I had in years, not that it's hard to rank all of them."

"I'm so happy for you, Essie," she says, taking my hand and lacing our fingers together. "So, what else did you do all day with your new time off?"

"I slept in and I went to the grocery store. Then, Brian came over and here we are. What are you doing home so early?"

"I thought you might want some help packing. I stopped by the liquor store and picked up a few empty boxes. I'd love to see your new place, even if I will be a little jealous of it."

I nod and climb off the couch, heading toward the front door to pull the boxes from her car. It would be nice to get a jumpstart on packing this place and start moving things slowly. I realize I'm going to need help from someone to get the bigger items since Petal can't lift anything heavy in her condition. I thought I would call Turner, but that's no longer an option. I wonder if Brian can help me.

We pack the boxes for a little while, spitballing ideas about what I could do for a living if I don't want to read fortunes. Petal sits down on the couch and puts one finger on each temple, making slow circles as she concentrates. "Let me think for a minute."

I pause my packing and sit down next to her, grateful for a break.

"What about a therapist?" she asks, and my mouth drops open. "What? Is that such a bad career move? You're good at listening to people, even when you don't want to be. Don't feel like you have to like it just because it's the first thing that came to my mind."

"It's not that," I explain. "It's just that it's the first thing Brian said too."

"Well, we can't *both* be wrong. He barely knows you and I know everything about you. If we both think the same thing, maybe it's a sign."

"I'll mull it over," I say, stacking the last box on top of the pile and collapsing beside Petal. "What will I do in the meantime though? It takes money to pay the bills while I'm in school."

"You could come work for me, just until you get your degree." She shrugs. "Think about it. What other job is going to be flexible enough that you can come and go around your classes, do homework in the downtime, and still get paid for a full-time salary?"

I have to admit that Petal's suggestion is appealing. As much as I hate reading fortunes and don't want to be in charge of an entire store, it *is* the best option if I'm serious about going back to school. That's at least two years of schooling depending on what I go back for, and I'm going to need a salary of some kind.

"Can I think about it?" I ask her.

"Take as much time as you need. Rose and I have it handled until you make a choice."

"I think I'm going to go to bed," I say, glancing at the clock that just struck nine. "Today has taken it out of me."

Petal laughs and throws a pillow at me. "You didn't even work today!"

"All the same," I laugh and make my way down the hall.

There's still one more thing I need to do to make things right for Petal. I think back to my four-step plan and realize I got hung up on step three of getting a good review. I have to find a way to remedy that.

Chapter 22

A week passes and Brian and I spend almost every waking minute together when he isn't at work. Even then, we text each other between his clients. When I realize I can't go back to The Glass Orb, he arranges for me to meet with a colleague who needs a receptionist in her office. Today is the day I find out just how screwed I am that my resume reads "fortuneteller" instead of "college grad." Brian suggests reframing my time as a psychic as time spent being an entrepreneur instead. This is stretching the truth because Petal is technically the owner, but I don't tell him that. Instead, I modify my resume and acknowledge that he's right.

He shoots me a text as I sit in the waiting room for my interview to begin. The room is far classier than any place I've ever worked before. Everything is clean with white walls and modern art, a few fresh plants sprinkled around the room. I remind myself to tell Petal what a difference a little bit of greenery makes and to gift her a plant when I successfully land a paying gig. My savings account is dangerously low without any income, and a plant is a splurge I can't afford without an identifiable paycheck rolling in. I almost laugh at the reversal of roles between Petal and me: she is now an entrepreneur with a somewhat steady paycheck while I'm an unemployed fortuneteller. Go figure.

"Esmerelda?" I look up to see a woman in ruby slacks and a flowing white shirt. Her straight hair is cut in a short bob, softened at the edges. She looks like the epitome of a successful businesswoman. It makes me feel like I'm underdressed in my navy-blue dress and I'm glad I wore my small wedge sandals to dress it up. If I get this job, I'll have to splurge on clothes to match her business casual attire.

I stand up and shake her hand, careful to apply firm pressure and to look her in the eye. I don't have the luxury of self-doubt because I need this job so desperately. I tell her how great it is to meet her and how highly Brian spoke of her. Rachel smiles and leads me down the hall to the room she must use to conduct sessions. She takes a seat in the plush armchair closest to the door while I awkwardly take a seat on the couch across from her.

"Tell me about your work history," she says, pulling my resume in front of her. "Brian told me you would be perfect, but he didn't tell me much about your history."

"Well," I start and pause. "I was an entrepreneur. My sister and I started a business together but it was her dream, not mine."

"And what kind of business was that?" She sits with a pen poised above my resume, ready to take notes. I imagine this is what she does during a session with a paying client.

I gulp and realize that this is going to be the common refrain if I'm not straightforward on my resume. With a sigh, I tell her the truth. "Fortunetelling."

"You were a psychic?"

I nod in response to her question and close my eyes to avoid seeing her response. When I open them, she is staring at me in interest rather than judgment.

"Tell me about that," she says, leaning forward in her chair. She's a good therapist. I can already tell.

I tell her a little more about how I learned to read people using everything on the table. We talk about the skills I had to learn, the perseverance it requires to start your own business, and even the courage it takes to walk away when you realize it doesn't fit into your plan for your life. Before I know it, twenty minutes passes and I feel like I aced the interview.

"I think you would be a perfect fit," Rachel says, standing up from her chair and setting my resume down on the desk behind her. "Would you be able to start on Monday? I'm in a bit of a bind since our last receptionist quit without warning."

"Monday is perfect," I tell her, without adding that there's nothing else I have to do since I'm currently unemployed. A steady paycheck is on the horizon. I'm not about to look this gift horse in the mouth. We shake hands and she escorts me back out to the lobby where she calls her next client back into her office.

I'm walking through the parking lot when I hear someone call my name. My first thought is that it must be Brian, here to see how my interview went. Then, I remember he was in a session with a client. I look around to see who could be calling my name: *Turner*.

And he isn't alone.

"Are you here to see Rachel, too?" he asks as he comes closer. Ryan looks less than pleased to have run into me here, but she trails behind him. "We've never run into you here before."

"I was here for an interview," I tell him.

"Thank God this is our last session with Rachel," Ryan says with a roll of her eyes. I don't know what the right thing to say is when you run into your ex and his new fiancée in the parking lot of a marriage counselor. Is good luck the wrong sentiment?

"Premarital counseling," Turner clarifies, turning around to take Ryan's hand. "It's one of the requirements our preacher has before he'll commit to marrying us."

"Six weeks of this finally at an end," Ryan offers.

I realize I have the perfect opportunity here and now to make a case for Petal. It would be an opportunity squandered not to convince Ryan to give The Glass Orb another chance. A new review would make a massive difference in client sentiment about the business, but I need this one to be positive. I have to play my cards extremely carefully here to flatter her without coming across as groveling for her help.

"I've been meaning to get in touch with you," I start and pause.

"If this is about the reviews, I'm not going to retract them," Ryan smirks and it makes me want to grab her perky blonde ponytail. Instead, I take a deep breath and say the one thing I know she would love to hear.

"Actually, I wanted to tell you that you were right to publish those articles. The Glass Orb *is* a scam." I keep my expression neutral, with no hint of a smile or frown for her to read.

"I'm glad you're coming around to the idea," she says, but she pauses. If nothing else, I've thrown her off her game. "Is that all you had to say?"

"Well, no. I *do* think what The Glass Orb offers is a sham because anybody can read tarot. It doesn't take someone special to flip over a couple of cards and say some mumbo jumbo. In fact, Petal's going to be teaching a class on how people can learn to do it for themselves." I shrug and try to gauge her reaction.

"I think I already covered the most interesting part of this story."

"I was wondering if you would be willing to cover the class – share our secrets with the rest of the world. This really benefits both of us."

"And I should do you a favor because?"

"You aren't doing *me* a favor. I don't work there and I'm not the one with my name on the lease. But Petal didn't do anything wrong here, and I don't see why she should suffer because you and I got off on the wrong foot."

"Are those flowers still on the table?" Ryan casts a pointed look at Turner.

"Those flowers are old news." I look her right in the eye. "They didn't mean a thing. But the opportunity for you to bust our secrets to the world could be good news for you."

"How does that benefit me?"

"I'm no reporter, but don't you have to pitch stories to your editor every week? Covering this aspect of spirituality and intuition is guaranteed content for a while. And trust me, there are far more people interested in how to 'tell the future' than you think."

She mulls it over for a moment, but Turner jumps in before she can respond.

"This is a great move for both of you," he says. "Ryan, they were just flowers and Ess just told you she doesn't work there anymore. In fact, she works *here* where we come for our *marriage* counseling."

"You want to tell me that there's nothing between you?" She turns her gaze back and forth between Turner and me, glaring. "I find out you've been meeting up behind my back and you want me to go along with this new plan of hers?"

"I helped her find an apartment, Ryan. It's literally my job – and reporting is yours. Ess is giving you an opportunity to have an extremely popular column and might give you the readership to take bigger assignments which is what you've wanted for years." He stops for a minute. "Don't punish Petal because I sent Esmerelda flowers for their opening day. It was literally a twenty-dollar bouquet of flowers for a client. It's even a business expense."

"*You* don't have to be involved?" Ryan turns her attention back to me, and I shake my head.

"I'll be too busy starting here to be anywhere near that class. Besides, what do I need to learn about telling the future?"

"Fine," Ryan says. "I'll pitch the idea. But I'm not doing it for you."

"I don't expect you to do anything for me." I take a few steps backward in the direction of my car. "Good luck to you on your last session."

I climb into the car and get behind the driver's wheel when my phone rings: Brian.

"Congratulations," he says cheerfully.

"How did you already know I got the job? You've been in a session with a client this whole time."

"Rachel texted me and I saw it as soon as my client left. I only have a few minutes between sessions, but I thought getting the job warranted a phone call instead of a text. When do you start?"

We talk about the details of my new job for a few minutes before he suggests that we get together tonight to celebrate this accomplishment.

"I should be in my new apartment tonight," I tell him. "Why don't you come over and I'll make dinner? I'm tired of takeout. It's all Petal and I have eaten while we've been moving places."

We agree on a plan and I have five hours until I see him. Ryan is safely in her marriage counseling session, which means there's no reason why I can't pop by The Glass Orb and share my good news with Petal. I know she's nervous about teaching this class with Rose, but she's been reading tarot for herself just as long as I've been doing it professionally. If I don't give her a little heads up that Ryan is coming, she's likely to get flustered and tongue-tied. I drive to the opposite side of town, listening to my music loudly in celebration.

"You'll never guess what happened," Petal exclaims as soon as I walk through the door.

"Yes, actually, I did ace my interview. Thanks for asking." I roll my eyes, but Petal is visibly excited about whatever has just happened.

"Right," she corrects, dampening her expression a little bit. "How did it go?"

"I start on Monday," I smile and raise two hands over my head like a cheerleader with pom-poms. "Now, what is *your* news?"

"Ryan just registered for our class on Friday," she says joyfully. "Maybe this time we can get a good review if we admit to everyone that there are no secrets about the tarot deck. It's going to be different than the last two times she can into the store. Plus, we'll know she's in the crowd and we can gauge her reaction as we go."

"I hate to say I know already, but who do you think convinced her to give it a second try?"

"You got in touch with her to get our review amended?"

"Actually, it was a fortuitous event," I say, trying to take on the air of a psychic. "I ran into her in the parking lot at my interview and convinced her to give you a shot now that I'm not the one working here anymore."

"You're the *best*!" Petal exclaims, rushing toward me to throw her arms around my neck. I can feel the slight bulge of her pregnant belly pressed against me as I hug her back. "I can't believe you did that for us."

Petal and I chat for a few minutes about the content and curriculum for her class. The class is designed to be taught over a four-week period. She has a pretty clear idea of where she wants it to go, and I'm in no place to criticize her decisions. This business is her baby, and she needs that leadership role. Eventually, I tell her I need to go get my place ready for Brian to come over tonight. She gives me a wolf whistle playfully as I back out the front door.

My new apartment is chaotic, but Brian and one of his friends helped me move most of the furniture. Petal still has my sleeper sofa until she buys a bed of her own. That means I have no place to sit in my new place other than the dining room table. When I walk through the front door, there are boxes stacked in every corner. With four hours left until Brian gets here, I start unpacking the boxes in the main living room as quickly as I can. My goal is simply to get as much out of the boxes as possible, break them down, and stack them neatly by the front door. He's already seen the place in various stages of dishevelment, but this is the first time we'll be *alone* in this apartment.

I'm very aware that our only options for seating are the dining room table and the bed.

Three hours pass and my bedroom is mostly put away with a decent dent in the living room. The kitchen has already been unpacked so I have my pots and pans to cook something for us to have for dinner. I open the refrigerator and look inside, realizing that I don't have much he'll really eat. Despite the success of the grown-up quesadillas, his tastebuds haven't changed much. I resolve to make peanut noodles which takes just one pot and, honestly, is a little bland. It will probably be a big hit with Brian.

I take the last hour to get date night ready. I take the braids out of my hair and shake out the loose curls, reapplying a layer of mascara and swiping on dark pink lipstick. I'm just coming out of the bathroom when he knocks at the front door. I swing it open wide and see that he's brought me a bouquet of daisies.

"A small congratulations gift," he shrugs, handing them over. "It was the least I could do since you were insistent on cooking tonight."

I take a step closer to him in the doorway until my lips brush his. This still feels like a new revelation every time we touch. There is a heat and an energy that courses through my body when our skin makes contact with each other. It can be as simple as holding hands or a long hug, but this kiss is just the start of our night.

"I was actually hoping we could do something kind of silly tonight," I tell him, walking back down the hall toward the kitchen where the noodles were being kept warm. "A little bit of a throwback to our first date."

"You want to go to the grocery store?"

"Okay, maybe not our first date. But the first time we *met* at least."

He takes a seat at the dining room table as I fuss with dinner on the stove. I pull out two bowls and use the pasta fork to ladle these long spaghetti noodles into individual servings. Brian takes a long look at the noodles in the bowl, then glances up at me.

"Should I ask what this is?"

"Peanut noodles," I tell him. "Don't knock it until you've tried it."

He takes a tentative bite and closes his eyes with a hum of praise. "Not bad, Essie. Anyway, you were saying?"

"I was hoping we could read your tarot cards tonight."

"You think tarot cards are a massive sham." He laughs. "What brought this on?"

"I was reminiscing this afternoon while unpacking those boxes and I had nostalgia when I found the deck Petal made for me. I was hoping you could be my guinea pig, for old time's sake."

"All right, let's have it." He sets his bowl to the side and clears the spot in front of him on the table. I pick the deck up where I left it and pass it to him to clear my energy away from it with a rose quartz crystal, instructing him to shuffle it when he's finished. He cuts the deck in thirds and then neatly stacks them into a single pile before handing it back to me.

"What does your love life hold?" I ask the deck, parroting the question he initially came to me with at The Glass Orb. I catch a glimpse of his smile just before I close my eyes and focus all of my attention on the deck in front of me. I can feel the energy buzzing from the middle of the deck, so I cut it in half until I get to the card that speaks to me. Sometimes, it feels like my intuition might be real, but it's so few and far between that I still think it's a sham.

"It seems silly to ask that question now," he says, but I shush him as I flip the card over.

'Ten of Cups,' I smile. "This card usually represents a happy ending, a love that stands the test of time."

"A good fortune," he says.

"Tell me, Brian. What do you think your happy ending is?"

He comes around the table with a smile and wraps his arms around me, pressing his lips to the side of my neck. I feel how sturdy and warm he is behind me, reaching up to lace my fingers with his. For the first time in a long time, I feel like I might have gotten my own happy ending: a new job, a better relationship with my sister, this fabulous new apartment, and Brian standing here in front of me with his lips against my skin.

This happy ending is more than I could have ever asked for.

About the Author

Ashley Loren is an avid storyteller and reader. When you find her without a book in her hands, she is drinking coffee with her husband, playing with her son, or working with her horses.

On the Table is her debut novel with its sequel, On the Map, coming out June 2024.

Subscribe to her Substack newsletter for details on preorders!
ashleylorenwrites.substack.com

Read more at ashleylorenwrites.com.

Milton Keynes UK
Ingram Content Group UK Ltd.
UKHW011223280324
440101UK00005B/553